HOTTER THAN SPELL

An Elemental Witches of Eternal Springs Cozy Mystery, Book 3

❦

ANNABEL CHASE

Red Palm Press LLC

Copyright © 2018 by Annabel Chase

All rights reserved.

No part of this book may be reproduced in any form or by any electronic or mechanical means, including information storage and retrieval systems, without written permission from the author, except for the use of brief quotations in a book review.

❦ Created with Vellum

Chapter One

"Where's my day planner?" I demanded, scouring the tabletops of the living room. When that search failed, I began lifting couch cushions. It was worse than hunting for the remote control. My house was only eighteen-hundred square feet and organized to the hilt. There was no excuse for anything to go missing.

The blue one or the orange one, miss? Gerald asked, fluttering into the room. Unlike most pink fairy armadillos, Gerald was an actual fairy version, complete with tiny pink wings. My familiar's main problem was that, thanks to a steady diet of hardboiled eggs and bacon, his body was slightly too heavy for his wings to lift him more than a foot or so off the ground. It wasn't unusual for me to find unpleasant evidence of Gerald's bottom dragging across the living room floor.

"The blue one," I said. "This is for work." My orange day planner was devoted solely to my social calendar. One was decidedly fuller than the other, but I won't say which one.

I believe it was on the kitchen counter last time I saw it. Next to the refrigerator.

"What were you doing in there?" I asked, hurrying into the kitchen to check. "Aha!" The blue planner was right beside the kettle on the stovetop. I should have known. Tea was usually my first port of call in the morning.

I may have been in the mood for an egg before bed last night, Gerald explained, trailing after me.

"Gerald, I told you before, we need to get you back to an insect- and plant-based diet. I will make you as many kale smoothies as you like, but you have to cut back on the eggs and bacon. It isn't good for you."

My familiar lowered his head in shame. *I do try, miss.*

"I know you do." I patted his head. "I'm not trying to make you feel bad about yourself."

Of course not, miss. You're much too kind.

I flipped to the tabbed page of the planner and scanned today's listings. "Eleven o'clock. That's what I thought."

Today was the first practice session for the big Battle of the Bands competition. As the island's director of tourism, I'm responsible for brainstorming ways to bring in more revenue from visitors. The jewel in the island's crown is the Eternal Springs Resort and Spa. Tourists come from far and wide to experience the famous mud pits. I'm not an all-eggs-in-one-basket kind of gal, so I was determined to expand our offerings during my tenure. Hosting a Battle of the Bands meant full hotel rooms, busy restaurants, and enormous bar tabs. If the competition went well, it would be the first of many. I also entertained grand visions of holding concerts in the canyon near the mud pits to rival Colorado's Red Rocks amphitheater. One goal at a time, though.

A suit today, miss? Gerald queried. *Are you sure that's the best choice?*

I glanced down at my navy blue suit. "You know what? You're right. It's band practice. I should wear something more appropriate, to blend in." My brow wrinkled. "Do I own any T-shirts, Gerald?"

No, miss, but I'm sure you can borrow one from Skye. She seems to have an endless supply of such garments.

I groaned at the mention of Skye Thornton. Skye and I are two of four witches left behind by our coven as the caretakers of the island. The other two—Zola and Evian—aren't nearly as irritating as Skye, though I wouldn't say they're my friends by choice. We were thrown together at St. Joan of Arc for our education and then, afterward, due to unfortunate circumstances. The "unfortunate circumstances" being the destruction of the school after a devastating fire, which may or may not have been the result of our negligence. Well, certainly not my negligence. Everybody knows I'm a stickler for rules and order. I would never have abandoned my post as a watcher of the other side. Some terrible creatures could—and sometimes did—enter our world through that gap if we aren't careful. And I'm always careful.

"I still need to look professional, Gerald. Half of Skye's wardrobe looks like it came straight from a high school locker." Complete with sweat stains.

Agreed, miss. Perhaps try your Helmut Lang silk tank and a pair of capris. Stylish yet casual.

"The black one?"

Silver, miss. With the ruched armholes. Pair them with your black capris.

I fist bumped my armadillo. "Good call, Gerald." I ran up the steps to my bedroom to change. I don't know what I'd do without my familiar. He's a fashion guru, spiritual advisor, best friend, and butler rolled into one chubby package.

I yanked open my closet door and scanned the floor for the right shoes. *Ballet flats or sandals?*

Depends on the state of your toenails, miss. You haven't been to see Sara in three weeks, by my calculations.

Ballet flats, it is.

I swapped my suit for more casual fare, ran a brush through my long dark hair and hustled downstairs.

Cup of tea? Gerald asked.

The alarm on the counter buzzed, indicating it was time for me to go.

"No time, but thanks," I replied. "Vegetable lasagna for dinner?"

I'm happy to do the necessary preparations, miss.

"You're the best." I grabbed my cross-body bag from the hook by the front door. "Hold down the fort, Gerald," I called over my shoulder.

As always, miss, he called back.

I stepped onto the front porch of my purple Craftsman house and was greeted by an albino raven perched on the edge of the Adirondack chair.

I gave him the stink eye. "What are you doing here, Stuart?"

"You know perfectly well what I'm doing here," Stuart replied. "Same as every other time."

"You need a hobby," I said. "Have you considered taking up knitting? I hear the needles don't even hurt if you stab yourself with one. You should try it."

He ignored me. "You're an amazing witch, Kenna, and you deserve an equally amazing familiar."

"And I suppose that's you." I continued down the porch steps to my white Vespa parked in the driveway. There are no cars on the island in order to preserve its character, so the only motorized transport available to residents are scooters and golf carts.

The pale raven flew after me. "That armadillo is useless. He can barely fly, whereas I'm able to leap tall buildings in a single go."

"We don't have any tall buildings on the island," I pointed

out. I strapped on my matching white helmet. I'm all about color coordination. "So I'm afraid your skill isn't really a selling point."

Stuart perched on the handlebars of my Vespa and cocked his head. "It's because I'm white, isn't it? If I were black like the other ravens, you'd be all over the idea."

"I wouldn't be all over anything because, as you are well aware, I already have a familiar." I started the motor, a signal to Stuart that I was ready to end the conversation.

"Gerald doesn't deserve you," he yelled.

But I was already halfway down the street.

Anchors Away is a beachside tiki bar with enough outdoor space to accomodate the bands as well as the anticipated audience. Although I'd received several bids from local bars to host the competition, Anchors Away ticked the most boxes, and was rewarded with the contract.

I was about to pull into the parking lot when I caught sight of a red and blue customized golf cart in the distance. The distinctive WW logo stood out clearly on the back.

"Waffle Wagon," I whispered. The Waffle Wagon is my white whale. The delicious liege-style Belgian waffles are only available on wheels, but there is no rhyme or reason to the schedule, which makes it impossible to pin down.

I glanced longingly at the wagon. If I gunned the engine of my scooter, I could make it before the wagon got away, but then I would be late for the practice session. I was the one in charge of the session, so I knew what my decision had to be. With an irritable grunt, I turned into the parking lot and parked my scooter next to the cleanest golf cart I could find. I tried to keep my white Vespa in pristine condition, and that meant parking far away from those who clearly didn't take pride in their vehicles.

"What's the occasion?" a deep voice asked.

I whipped around and stared right into a bare chest. Granted, it was an incredibly nice chest, with defined muscles and admirable pecs, but it was still a naked man chest. At eleven o'clock in the morning.

"The occasion?" I repeated. My gaze traveled up to his attractive face. His dark blond hair caught the sunlight, and, for a brief moment, I forgot where I was and what I was doing.

The bark of a dog brought me back to earth. A huge black and white Great Dane stood beside him.

"Aren't you stunning?" I said, admiring the sleek body of the dog. "Her coloring is so unusual."

"She's a harlequin Dane," he said. "Her name's Leia."

"Nice to meet you, Leia. You're a beauty."

"She certainly is," Naked Man Chest said.

I couldn't bring myself to look back at him and his flawless body. "I need to get to work. There's a practice session today for the Battle of the Bands competition. Have you heard about it?"

"No, but it sounds great. I'll bet it was your idea, wasn't it?"

I wasn't usually shy and reserved, but I found myself staring at his running shoes. "It was, actually. How'd you know?"

"Kenna," someone called from the bar area. "Thank God you're here. We need you. One of the speakers isn't working."

"Duty calls," I said. "It was nice chatting with you." As much as I would have loved to continue my conversation with Naked Man Chest, I had work to do.

Despite the morning hour, the bar teemed with people. I caught sight of Captain Mack Shakes working up a sweat behind the bar. I had warned him to hire extra help for the event. Hopefully, he'd decide to listen to me after this practice session. There was no guarantee, as my recommendations often fell on deaf ears. It was amazing I managed to do my job as well as I did. I was the island's very own Cassandra, my warnings of doom and disaster summarily dismissed. I'd also advised Mack to skip his usual drunken Johnny Depp shtick that he lapsed into whenever tourists were around. The bands weren't interested in anything except music, alcohol and attractive women.

"Good morning, Mack," I said, resting my elbows on the bar. "How's everything going?"

"Busier than I'd expect for a Tuesday morning," he said. "We don't ever see this kind of crowd so early, not even during the high season."

I smiled. "You're welcome."

"I think you're right about the extra hands," Mack said. "I'll definitely have extra help here for the actual competition."

"Good plan." I surveyed the scene. "Looks like all the bands that signed up for the practice session are here." A few bands weren't coming to the island until closer to the competition due to scheduling conflicts.

"Oh, they're here," he said. "And very thirsty." He pulled a few pints and slid them down the end of the bar. "Can I get you anything?"

"No, thanks." I pretended to roll up my sleeves. "I'm here to work."

"Do you ever do anything else?" Mack queried.

I shot him a look of surprise. "Of course."

He wore an amused look. "Name something."

"I...watch television," I said. I hoped he didn't ask me what shows because Mitzi's knitting program was really the only one I ever watched, and that was in order to zone out.

Mack dropped his voice. "Maybe it's time you start dating. A relationship might be good for you."

I flashed a smile. "Mack, I appreciate you looking out for me, but I'm not one of your barflies. You don't need to counsel me or offer me sage advice. I'm a grown woman and I can take care of myself."

"I know you are, Kenna, but wouldn't it be nice to let someone else take care of you, if only every once in a while?"

A noise from the makeshift stage grabbed my attention. "Ooh, the first band is about to start."

Mack peered over my shoulder. "I recognize the lead singer. That's Fat Gandalf. They've played here before."

I studied the tall, lean man on stage. He wore a sleeveless top that showed off his sinewy muscles.

"They're local, right?" I asked.

"Sure are. Favorable odds for winning the competition, too," Mack said. "Not that I'm a betting man."

The lead singer tapped the end of his microphone. "Pete, you out there?"

Heads swiveled as everyone scanned the area for Pete.

"We can't start without you," the singer said. "Kinda need those drums."

My body tensed. Fat Gandalf was first. If their set started late, that would throw off the schedule for the entire day. A disaster in the making.

"I can't have this," I muttered. I strode toward the stage, my jaw set. As my feet sank into the sand, I was grateful to Gerald for suggesting ballet flats. Heels would have been a problem.

The lead singer continued to call for the drummer, Pete. The bassist and lead guitarist were on the stage as well, staring absently at each other.

"I need you guys to start," I said, tapping the imaginary watch on my wrist. "Otherwise, you'll throw off the whole practice schedule."

A woman hurried to the stage, her blond ponytail

swinging behind her. It seemed too early for groupies to rush the stage.

"I'm sorry, miss," I said. "The stage is for band members only."

"This is my wife, Rachel. She's the manager for Fat Gandalf," the lead singer said.

She extended her hand. "Rachel Simonson."

As a self-proclaimed feminist, I was mortified to have mistaken her for a groupie.

"I'm sorry," I said. "The stress is already getting to me."

"I know how you feel," she said. "I was under the impression we were fourth in the practice session. It was Keith who insisted they were first." She rifled through her tote bag and produced a blue day planner identical to mine. "I usually make very detailed notes of the band's schedule."

"I have the same planner," I said, brightening.

"I can't live without mine," Rachel declared. "Keith thinks I'm ridiculous, but it generally keeps everything running smoothly."

"Speaking of running smoothly," I said, "we really need to get started."

"We can't start without Pete," Keith said. "The drummer is the backbone of the band."

I glanced around in exasperation. "What does he look like? I'll find him. You just start and do the best you can without him."

"Brown hair, wearing a Charlie Brown T-shirt," Keith said.

"Okay, Gandalf," I said. "I'm on it."

"It's Keith," he replied. "Keith Simonson. The *band* is called Fat Gandalf."

"Oh, right." I shook my head in an effort to get my thoughts in order. "I'll be back with Charlie Brown."

"Let me know if you need any help," Rachel called after me. "I hate being idle."

I hustled off the stage and began combing the outdoor area before moving to the interior of Anchors Away. I asked anyone I passed if they'd seen a man in a Charlie Brown T-shirt. What passed for fashion these days was disappointing.

"I saw that guy in the bathroom," a longhaired, bearded man said.

"When?"

The man scratched his beard. "Earlier."

"How much earlier?" I asked impatiently. "Ten minutes ago? An hour?"

The man nodded slowly. "Time is a manmade construct, you know?"

Oh boy. We had a live one. "Charlie Brown T-shirt," I repeated.

"In the bathroom," he said again.

I kept walking, poking my head in and out of places and calling Pete's name. Finally, I decided to check the restrooms, just to be thorough. The ladies' room was clear, so I headed to the men's room.

"Pete," I called from the open doorway. No answer. I really didn't want to go inside. The mere thought of the germs and filth was enough to make me reach in my cross-body bag for an antacid.

There was no one around, so I couldn't ask for help. I inhaled deeply before holding my breath and venturing inside.

"Pete?" There was no one at the urinals—thank Goddess. I checked the first stall. Empty. I inched over to the second stall, but the door was closed.

"Excuse me," I said, knocking. "Are you Pete?" The door swung open but stopped short, like something was blocking it. There was no response from inside.

"Pete?"

I pushed harder and the gap widened as something

collapsed onto the floor in a heap. I recognized the telltale yellow and black shirt of Charlie Brown.

"Oh, no. Pete, is that you?"

There was no answer because, of course, the dead don't speak.

Chapter Two

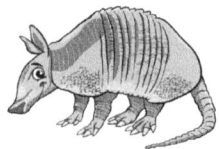

"Yes, he's definitely dead." Dr. Abigail Marley stood over the body in the stall of the men's room and nudged it with the toe of her strappy sandal. You know a town is small and superficial when its medical examiner doubles as a plastic surgeon in the local spa's world-renowned plastic surgery wing.

"Thank you for your keen assessment," I said.

Abigail faced me. "Speaking of keen assessments, it wouldn't be the worst thing in the world if you made an appointment with my office."

I worked hard to suppress my irritation. "And why would I do that?"

She touched my forehead. "Too much frowning, Kenna. You need to try less expression."

"I'm thirty," I said. "It's a little too soon to be concerned."

"Never too soon, Kenna. A little Botox injection and you'll be fighting them off."

"I don't want to have to fight anyone off." That sounded immensely unappealing.

She shrugged. "Take it from me, your shelf life is shorter than you think. It's good to take measures to extend it."

"Wouldn't have helped this guy," I said, gesturing to Pete. "How did he die?"

"That's where the examiner part of my job kicks in," Dr. Marley replied.

"Looks like a nasty bruise on his head," I said. The skin was purple and swollen. He must've hit it hard on the edge of the toilet.

"I'm guessing drugs," Abigail said.

"You're guessing *drugs*? Why, just because he was the drummer in a band?" Talk about biased.

"No, because of the bag of drugs on the floor there." She pointed to the floor and I crouched down to see a small plastic bag in the next stall.

Oh. "He must have dropped it," I said.

"Don't touch it," she snapped. "We need to preserve the evidence."

"I know," I said quickly. "I wasn't going to touch it." Actually, I *was* going to pick it up off the floor. It was a compulsion, though. If there was a bag on the floor that didn't belong there, I needed to fix it.

"Buddy is on his way," Dr. Marley said. "He'll want to see the evidence as it was discovered."

"Tell him Pete's drumsticks are there too," I said. I'd moved to the third stall, where the drumsticks were scattered on the floor.

"Did someone say drumsticks? Now I'm hungry." Barnaby Sterling Montgomery, or Buddy as he liked to be called, waddled his way into the restroom. Buddy served as the mayor, the chief of police, the senior center president and the water department chief. He wasn't necessarily effective at all these jobs, but he liked amassing titles. For some reason, the residents of Eternal Springs allowed it.

"Not those kind of drumsticks," I said. "The kind an actual drummer uses."

Buddy looked disappointed, and I briefly worried that he would have eaten chicken drumsticks fresh off the bathroom floor if they'd been available.

"His name is Pete," I said. "He's the drummer for Fat Gandalf." The band was outside with no idea what happened to their bandmate.

"I recognize him," Buddy said. "Pete Simpson. His company's done electrical work in my house."

"His company?" I echoed.

"He owns an electrical company with his brother," Buddy said. "Must be his day job."

"Not anymore," Abigail said.

"So what's the theory?" Buddy asked.

"He came into the bathroom to do drugs before his performance," Abigail said. "He got so high on cocaine that he tried to drink out of the toilet and hit his head. Or maybe he was so delusional from the cocaine that he tried to stick one of his drumsticks up his nose instead of the coke."

I balked. "Is this how you normally work? There's no cocaine, only pot."

"A minor detail," Abigail said dismissively. "Drugs are drugs."

"Abigail's excellent at working through her theories," Buddy said.

"Shouldn't she be excellent at working through facts based on the actual medical examination?" I asked. "Last time I checked, you don't stick pot up your nose."

Buddy appraised me. "Sounds like you speak from personal experience."

I straightened. "Do I seem like the kind of person who smokes pot?"

"No, but you seem like the kind of person who definitely should."

I whirled around to see Skye hovering near the urinals. "Go away, Skye. This is none of your business."

"This doesn't strike me as your usual hangout," Skye said.

"Why don't you escort your nosy friend out of here, Kenna?" Buddy said. "I'm sure the bands out there are in dire need of direction from you about now."

He wasn't wrong. Not to mention the restroom was becoming a bit too crowded for my taste.

I grabbed Skye by the elbow and steered her out of the men's room.

"What are you doing here, Skye?" I eyed my coven sister carefully. She owned and was the sole reporter for The Town Croaker and a general busybody. The last thing I wanted was for word to get out about Pete. It would freak out the participants.

"Heard there's a meeting in the ladies' room," she said. "And I'll be back real soon."

At the sound of '80s lyrics, my gaze narrowed. Skye knew how I felt about funk music. I was more of a power ballad girl.

I drew a deep breath of fresh air in an attempt to steady my nerves. "Feel free to use the ladies' room," I said. "Nowhere else should be of interest to you."

"Is it true there's a dead body in there?" She moved to get around me, but I blocked her path.

"Leave it, Skye," I ground out. "There's nothing to report." Yet.

Skye stood on her tiptoes to try to peer over my shoulder. That was the benefit of being a good three inches taller than her.

"I know Buddy's in there," she said. "Not that you can

miss him. It's like watching an eclipse. Did I see the fancy shoes of Dr. Abigail Marley in the stall?"

"Go away, Skye," I said, wriggling my fingers. "Or I'll singe off those beloved eyebrows of yours. They're so pale, no one would notice anyway."

Skye twitched. When I threatened to use my magic, she knew I meant business. We're elemental witches and my specialty is fire. Skye's specialty is air. Technically, she could suck all the oxygen away and destroy my fire, but, most of the time, she didn't react fast enough. My reflexes gave me a distinct advantage over her.

"Fine," Skye said, relenting. "I'll go back and cover the bands. For now." She blew a short blast of air in my direction for good measure, just enough to mess up my hair.

"Witch," I hissed.

Skye smiled. "And don't you forget it."

I followed her back to the sandy area where Fat Gandalf had been replaced on the stage by a band called Pigs in Blankets.

I spotted the lead singer and the other bandmates by the bar. Keith's arm was slung around the shoulders of a blond woman. His brow lifted when he saw me.

"You find him?" he asked. "Eric and Steve have a bet going." He pointed to the bassist and lead guitarist, respectively.

"I saw Dr. Marley rush through," Steve said. "Is he hurt?"

Holy Olivia Newton-John. No one had told them yet. I assumed word had leaked out, especially with the arrival of Abigail and Buddy. Then again, those two were seen together under a variety of circumstances—the resort, the golf course, the municipal building. The duo didn't automatically signify 'death.'

"Steve has twenty bucks on a slip and fall," Keith said.

"He is the clumsiest one of us," Steve said with a laugh. "I keep waiting for him to electrocute himself at work."

"My money's on sleep," Eric said. "He's been running himself ragged between the band and his day job. That guy can sleep anywhere. I've woken him up in the middle of a rave."

"Um, I found Pete, and he definitely wasn't asleep." I flagged down Mack. "Could I please have an Aperol spritz?"

Mack frowned. "You sure about that?"

The bartender knew I rarely drank on the job. "Just one, Mack. Thank you."

"So where is he then?" Keith polished off his beer and focused on me.

"I'm afraid he's..." Mack handed me the drink and I downed it. "Dead."

Everyone gaped at me.

"What do you mean?" Eric asked.

I swallowed hard. "I'm really sorry. Pete's dead. The medical examiner and the chief of police are with him now. I'm sure they'll release a statement when they have enough information. In the meantime, please keep this to yourselves. We don't want to upset people."

Rachel burst into tears. "This isn't real. We were just with him earlier this morning."

Keith squeezed her against him. "It's okay, honey. We'll find out what happened."

Eric lowered his head. "The timing sucks. How are we supposed to get another drummer on short notice? The competition is just around the corner."

"Eric, show some respect," Steve said. "The lady just told us Pete died and you're upset about a music competition." He shook his head in disgust.

"Can we see him?" Keith asked, craning his neck as though he could glimpse Pete in the distance.

"The area is cordoned off now," I said. "They're preparing the body for transport."

Keith buried his head in his hands. "This is a nightmare. Poor Pete."

Rachel gripped her husband's arm. "Oh, God. Someone needs to tell Tiffany."

"His girlfriend?" I queried.

"His wife," Eric corrected.

"And Mike and Lizzie," Steve added. "This is unreal." He appeared as dazed as he sounded.

Eric grimaced. "We sounded awful without a drummer up there. We've got to find someone quickly."

"Eric, if you mention another drummer again, I'm going to knock your teeth out," Steve warned.

Rachel laid a perfectly manicured hand on Steve's shoulder. "Let's not turn on each other. We need to come together now more than ever." Rachel turned to me. "That being said, we'll find another drummer in time. Please keep us on the roster."

"Pete would want us to compete," Keith said, his head bobbing. "He thought our chances of winning this were high."

Steve sniffed. "He believed in us."

Rachel squeezed his shoulder. "I still believe in you guys, but let's take a moment, okay? We just lost our Pete."

Keith nodded slowly. "We did. We lost our Pete."

The husband and wife put their arms around each other and the other bandmates followed suit.

"I think this calls for shots," Eric said. "I'll get the first round."

That was my cue to excuse myself. There was far too much to do to get sucked into a grief-inspired drinking spiral.

I said my goodbyes and turned back toward the stage,

where the next band was setting up. As I crossed the sand, I spotted the hot shirtless guy from the parking lot, only now he looked freshly showered in shorts and a T-shirt. He grinned when he saw me.

"That last band sounded pretty good," he said, coming toward me.

"Did they?" I said vaguely. "Oh, I'm glad."

He frowned. "Aren't you supposed to be paying attention? I thought this was your event."

"Where's Leia?" I asked.

"I took her home and grabbed a quick shower before I came back to check things out." He folded his arms and gave the place an approving nod. "Looks like everything's going well."

"Not exactly," I said. Wait. Why was I admitting this to a stranger? I wanted to keep Pete's death as quiet as possible.

The hot guy focused on me. "Is everything okay, Kenna?"

I opened my mouth to respond and then snapped it closed. He knew my name? "Do we know each other?"

"I'm Lucas Holmes," he said. "We graduated high school together. You came senior year with your three friends."

Lucas. Leia. My brain was ready to explode. "Skywalker?" My voice was a near whisper.

Lucas chuckled. "I haven't heard that name in years. It's pretty much Lucas 24/7 now."

I wasn't sure I ever knew his real name. The other witches and I had dubbed him Skywalker when we caught him in the Cottonmouth Copse playing alone with his lightsaber...and, no, that's not a euphemism. He was actually battling trees with a glowing lightsaber. We still attended St. Joan of Arc at the time—it was before the fire. When we arrived at the local high school, we recognized him and proceeded to torment him during our brief tenure. We used our magic to leave photographs of Darth Vader that read 'I am your father' everywhere he went—his locker, the gym locker room, even the urinal in the boys' bathroom. By the time we graduated, everyone was calling him Skywalker. He was so gawky then, nothing like the Adonis that stood before me now. To this day, he had no idea that we were responsible for his humiliation.

"I'm sorry," I said. "Skywalker was the first name that sprang to mind." Yet he knew my name. That fact somehow made it worse.

"I didn't love the nickname at the time," he admitted. "But I'm thirty now, so I've kind of embraced my inner geek. And I'm still a *Star Wars* fan."

"Leia," I said, and he nodded.

"Truth be told, I am, too," I said. "My friend Skye and I used to have the movies on constant rotation. We annoyed Zola and Evian to no end." I smiled at the memory. Sometimes the other witches and I got along; at least we had our moments. With four different personalities in the mix, we were bound to get on each other's nerves. Not to mention our banishment to the island. I think we often took our frustration out on each other because we could.

"Kenna, someone's looking for you," a reedy guy said. I didn't know his name.

"Be right there," I said, my gaze still fixed on Lucas.

"Looks like you need to get back to work," Lucas said. "I'm sorry to interrupt."

I gave a dismissive wave. "No, it's fine. It's already been a horrible day and it's barely begun."

Lucas appeared genuinely concerned. "Anything I can help with?"

I inclined my head, touched by the offer. Another wave of guilt threatened to overwhelm me. We tortured this gorgeous guy for months out of pure bitchiness, and here he was, offering himself as a knight in shining armor.

"No, thank you," I finally said. "That's kind of you, though."

He grinned and my heart skipped a beat. "I like to make myself useful," he said.

"Me, too," I said. "I get itchy if I have nothing to do."

"How would you know?" he asked good-naturedly. "You seem to always be in motion."

Wow. He seemed to be pretty observant. How on earth had I missed seeing him around town? At six foot four and full of handsome with a Great Dane sidekick, he couldn't be invisible if he tried.

"Do you...work on the mainland?" I asked. It didn't seem likely, but that was the only conclusion I could reach.

"Sort of," he said. "I'm a pilot."

My mouth formed a tiny 'o.'

He must have sensed my apprehension. "You have something against pilots?"

"No, I have something against leaving the ground," I said. "I'm a big fan of gravity." I didn't even fly on a broomstick, though I could if I were so inclined. Skye was the most willing. Then again, she was a witch of the wind. It suited her more.

"Kenna." My name echoed around us. Someone was using the microphone to summon me.

"I need to go," I said. "It was nice talking to you."

"See you around."

On my way to the stage, I glimpsed the covered gurney as it was carried out of the bar. Fortunately, people were so caught up in the buzz of activity around them that they failed to notice. My stomach dropped. A man died at my event. If I hadn't arranged the practice session, he might still be alive. I couldn't pretend that it didn't bother me. I was an overachiever since the day I was born with a full head of hair and set of teeth. An incident like this on my watch was unacceptable.

I needed to know what had happened to Pete Simpson and why.

Chapter Three

You seem out of sorts, miss, my observant familiar said. *Did the practice session not go as planned?*

I'd arrived home that evening and immediately plopped onto the couch, ready to sink into a coma.

"You could say that. Someone died today," I said.

Forgive me for stating the obvious, miss, but someone dies every day, Gerald said. *It's the cyclical nature of living things.*

"I found him," I said quietly. "Buddy and Abigail want to pretend it was accidental for the sake of the town, but he was definitely murdered."

I'd spoken to both of them later in the day, and they were insistent on sticking with the story that it was a drug-related accident. At least they had to run a toxicology report. If the results came back clean, they'd be forced to launch an investigation. The problem was that it could take a week for the results. In the meantime, there was a murderer running loose on the island. Naturally, it had to be the week leading up to my big event.

Oh, dear. That's dreadful. Gerald fluttered over to rest on the adjacent couch cushion. *A murder at Anchors Away? How is it even possible?*

"I don't know, but I have to find out," I said. "There's no way he did this to himself. The position of the body...It looked like he was attacked from behind."

So you don't believe it was an accident? Perhaps a drug overdose?

"No way. The bag of pot was unopened. We don't even know if it was his. Maybe he was holding it for someone." Now I sounded like the teenager who blames her friend when she gets caught with a half-empty bottle of vodka.

Are you certain you're equipped to investigate a murder, miss? Gerald squinted his little armadillo face at me. *I mean, I'm the first to praise your capabilities, but this is far different from organizing a tour of the mud pits for visiting dignitaries.*

"I know, Gerald, but I can't let laziness win the day."

Buddy's laziness, I take it?

"Exactly." Buddy was the type of man who'd wear a diaper on a cross-country journey, just to avoid walking from the car to the bathroom. Abigail, on the other hand, wasn't lazy, just incompetent.

I'm sorry your day was unpleasant, miss.

A smile tugged at my lips. "It wasn't all bad, to be honest. There was one silver lining."

Gerald flew around me in a circle. *Do tell, miss. That sounds encouraging.*

I plucked an imaginary loose thread on the couch. "Do you remember Skywalker?"

Gerald landed on the rug in front of me with a gentle thud. *The young Jedi-in-training from the Cottonmouth Copse?*

I bit back a smile. "Yes, that's him. It turns out he grew up to be an incredibly handsome pilot." I retrieved a mental image of his droolworthy man chest. A woman could feast on that image for months, maybe even a lifetime. "He seems to know who I am."

If I recall correctly, you and your sister witches enjoyed quite a bit of fun at his expense. Does he know it was you?

I pressed my lips together.

Your silence suggests not. No matter, miss. It was many years ago and I'm sure you'll be forgiven once you confess.

"Confess?" I wasn't even sure if or when I'd see him again. He'd managed to elude me this long on the island. Why plan on a confession?

Well, forgive me for saying so, but you seem a bit smitten with him, Gerald said. *If that's the case, you'll want to start a relationship with him on the right foot.*

I froze. "A relationship? Who said anything about a relationship? I just mentioned that I met a hot guy. No need to book the reception venue."

And when was the last time you've made such a mention?

"Um, never."

Exactly my point, miss. Young Skywalker must be something special to catch your attention. You're often so laser-focused on your tasks.

"Don't call him that," I said. "His name is Lucas Holmes, and he seems really nice." And hot. Did I mention his scorching hotness? As a fire witch, I greatly appreciate that quality in a man.

How do you intend to proceed with the murder investigation? Gerald asked. *I'm here to assist you, as always.*

"I'm not sure yet, but I'll let you know." The mention of Pete's murder put me right back in my funk. Even thoughts of Lucas's blue eyes weren't enough to lift my spirits. I closed my eyes and exhaled softly. Maybe a good night's sleep would do the trick.

Which shall it be then, miss? Bonnie Tyler or Mitzi?

Gerald knows me so well. When I'm having a difficult day, I choose one of two paths—one is '80s power ballads. Bonnie's *Total Eclipse of the Heart*, Journey's *Don't Stop Believin'*,

Heart's *Alone*, and Night Ranger's *Sister Christian* are my go-to's. I sing them as loud and passionately as I can—sometimes I even stand in the shower—without the water turned on—just for the acoustics. Gerald generally has the good sense to flee the house for half an hour for the sake of his little armadillo eardrums.

I pulled my knees to my chest. "I think I'm going to go with Mitzi on this one."

Excellent choice, miss, he said, and turned on the radio.

I stared blankly at the wall, waiting for the show to start. It was a mind-numbingly boring local show—*Knitter's Circle with Mitzi Montgomery*. Mitzi, Buddy's much younger wife, is almost as annoying as her husband. She's an obsessive knitter, probably a coping device to avoid her grating husband. If he wasn't careful, one of these days she might lose her patience and stab him with one of those knitting needles. Anyway, indulging in the show was my little secret. I use it to relax after a stressful day, not that I would ever admit it to anyone. Skye would never let me live it down. The fact that she knows about the power ballads is bad enough.

Mitzi yammered on about the variety of yarn colors, but my brain refused to calm. It was firing on all cylinders, the image of Pete on the bathroom floor burned into my retinas. I had to come up with a plan to solve the murder. Mitzi's description of what was certainly an ugly knitted scarf wouldn't help me with that. I tuned out the show and rose to my feet.

Cup of tea, miss? Gerald offered.

"No, thanks, Gerald," I said. "I'm going to take a shower and then go to bed. I'm exhausted." Physically and emotionally.

The armadillo appeared alarmed. *A shower?*

"Not to sing, Gerald. To think." And wash off the stench of death, not to mention the Anchors Away men's room.

He relaxed slightly. *Sounds like a good idea.*

I trudged up the stairs, turning the morning's events in my mind. If Buddy and Abigail were going to find excuses not to investigate, no one else would pick up the slack unless the family demanded it. Someone with a stake in the outcome. Like me. I couldn't afford to have a killer running around the island in advance of the competition. It could ruin the big event, and I'd worked months to make this a success. My selfish reasons aside, Pete deserved better. His killer had to be brought to justice. As much as I wanted to turn the other cheek and focus on my own job, I knew finding out what really happened was the right thing to do. I'd turned the other cheek once and it had resulted in disaster. I'd never do it again.

In my bedroom, I opened the dresser drawer and immediately noticed the abhorrent mix of colors. It looked like an underwear massacre.

"Gerald!" I yelled.

He fluttered into the room, huffing and puffing, his bottom dragging on the floor. He really did need to think about a diet. His butt was going to get carpet burns.

Yes, miss?

"What happened to my drawer?" I asked.

Gerald peered inside. *Oh, dear. Yes, I forgot to mention...*

"You forgot to mention what? Gerald, why are you rooting around in my underwear drawer?" It was uncomfortable on so many levels.

It's not what you think, miss. I've been trying to help you organize.

I closed the drawer and looked at him. "I appreciate the effort, Gerald, I really do, but whatever you're doing isn't working. It's an eyesore in there." I pressed my fingertips to my temples. "I think I feel a migraine coming on."

I'll fetch your ibuprofen and a glass of water.

"Thank you. If you leave it downstairs, I'll take it after my shower." I needed ten minutes of peace and quiet. I adored Gerald, but sometimes I just wanted to be alone.

I went into the bathroom and closed the door. My gaze drifted to the toilet and I pictured Pete's body on the floor. Abigail and Buddy's assumptions were wrong. I knew it in my gut. His pants had still been fastened. It didn't appear as though he'd been using the facilities. Not yet anyway. Someone had caught him off guard.

I turned on the water, the gears in my mind clicking away. There were so many possibilities. Pete's brother would be a good place to start, though. If the two brothers worked together, then they were probably close, so Mike would know if Pete had any enemies. Not to mention—if Mike was deeply unhappy about Pete's decision to leave their company, that was a solid motive for murder.

As I showered, I felt a song rise in my throat. With a mental apology to Gerald, I began to belt out the lyrics to *Sister Christian*. It seemed appropriate. Although I didn't know him, somehow, I knew Pete would have appreciated my choice.

I WOKE EARLIER THAN USUAL, READY TO START THE DAY. IF I was going to fit a murder investigation into my already-packed schedule. I needed to rise to the occasion.

Gerald was unprepared for my change in plans. He fluttered anxiously around the kitchen, muttering about unionizing.

"Just a banana for now, Gerald," I said. "I'm heading to the forest before I go to the office. I'm going to make like a Girl Scout and be prepared."

When you say the forest, do you mean the Cottonmouth Copse?

I shrugged. "It's the only place to gather cackleberries." If

I intended to interview potential suspects, the cackleberrries might come in handy. The key ingredient in truth serum, they only grew in this small area on the island.

Zola should have the fruit available. Why not try her shop?

"Zola and I aren't on the best terms right now." Zola is the earth witch in our elemental group.

You only need tell her you weren't involved.

"What's the point? She always believes Skye." Skye had recently played a prank on Zola and made sure to frame me as the guilty party. More bang for her witchy tricks. I'd been too busy to defend my honor, so I knew Zola was probably plotting her revenge.

Then I shall accompany you to the copse, miss. Those trees can be quite nasty.

"That won't be necessary. I can handle the trees. They're all talk and no action."

Then I shall come simply for the pleasure of your company.

"Fine." There was no point in arguing. The sun was shining and we were alive. I decided to focus on that.

I placed Gerald in the basket of my scooter and backed out of the driveway. Despite my helmet, I heard the loud flapping wings.

"Good morning, Stuart," I said, not bothering to glance to my left.

"An expedition, is it? I'm available to join."

"I'm not Christopher Robin and we are not headed into the Hundred Acre Wood," I said.

"Oh, I love *Winnie the Pooh*," Stuart exclaimed. "Are you a fan?"

I groaned and continued driving. Stuart flew along beside us.

I don't trust him, miss. He may try to off me while we're in the forest.

You can defend yourself, Gerald, I replied. *Your magic is impressive in its own right.*

"Where are we going?" Stuart asked. "It's the Cottonmouth Copse, right? I knew it. You're hunting for cackleberries."

"Pipe down, Stuart," I said. "You never know who's within earshot."

I fixed him with my hard stare. "You really know more than you should."

"Then you may as well use it to your advantage," Stuart said.

I parked my scooter in a clearing and hung my helmet on the handlebars by its strap. "You know what? I will. Your job is to be the lookout. If anyone comes while Gerald and I are gathering berries, sound the alarm."

"Like this?" Stuart let loose an ear-splitting noise that made me wince in pain.

"Maybe less blatant," I said. "Fly above the trees so you can see further afield. Gives us more lead time."

"Aye, aye, Captain Kenna." Stuart saluted me with his wing and flew off.

I winked at Gerald. "That takes care of him. I mean, no one ever comes here except us witches."

I couldn't avoid the sarcastic trees, not if I wanted cackleberries. Only the trees near the Blathering Brook housed the souls of the dead. That's why we witches call it the Cottonmouth Copse. Thankfully, we're the only people who can hear their chatter. It took a rather confident personality to stave off their abuse.

"As I live and breathe," Agatha said.

"You may live," I said, "but you certainly don't breathe."

"I rely on oxygen, same as you," Agatha countered. "That qualifies as breathing."

"If you say so."

"What happened to you anyway?" Agatha asked. "You were a lot prettier the last time I saw you."

I whipped around, ready to hurl my basket at her trunk.

"Never mind them, Kenna," Earl said. Hands down, he was the nicest tree in the copse. Well, he was the only nice tree in the copse. "I think you look like a young Elizabeth Taylor fresh off the set of *Cleopatra* set."

I swung my dark hair over my shoulder. "Thank you, Earl."

The other trees made kissing noises.

"Why don't you just marry her, Earl?" Myra jeered. "Have ten little saplings and live happily ever after?"

I ignored the trees and began the search for cackleberries, parting every potential bush in sight.

"If you're looking for cackleberries, I'm afraid you're out of luck," Earl said.

I straightened. "Why? What happened?"

"Skye came through here not so long ago," Agatha said. "Her and that inappropriate mouth of hers."

"She cleaned out the remaining cackleberries," Myra said.

"I wish she'd clean out her mouth with soap," Agatha added.

I smacked my forehead. I knew exactly when that had happened. Skye had accidentally fed us truth serum at Coconuts one night. The after-effects still made my head pulse with pain when I thought about it too much.

Gerald began flying over the more difficult-to-reach bushes. *Let me investigate these areas. Skye may have missed some.*

"Even if she did, we need a lot," I said.

"Incoming," Stuart shrieked. He zoomed through the trees, nearly colliding with one of Myra's branches.

"Incoming?" I queried. "You can't be serious. Who on earth...?" There was no time to finish the question.

"Ooh, it's Skywalker," Myra cooed. "I love it when he comes to visit."

Sure enough, Lucas Holmes entered the copse, looking as shocked to see me as I was to see him. Gerald dropped to the ground as if he'd been smacked down by gravity.

"Your armadillo is so cool," he said.

"What are you doing here, Lucas?" I asked.

"He's checking out your boobs, that's what he's doing," Myra said.

Agatha sniffed. "He'd need a magnifying glass for those mosquito bites."

"They're solid grapefruits," I said heatedly.

"Maybe even cantaloupes, depending on where you are in your cycle," Earl added.

I cringed as the trees cackled.

Lucas's brow creased. "I don't think you'll find grapefruits here. Just some weird berries." He surveyed the area. "Though I don't see any now."

"Where's Leia?" I asked.

"I left her home," he said. "This is where I come to...to..."

Play with your lightsaber, I nearly said. This was the spot where we'd caught him, all those years ago.

"He's a regular," Agatha said. "We see him all the time."

"He's the highlight of my week," Myra said.

"A line of ants in front of your trunk is the highlight of your week," Agatha said. "That's not saying much."

Lucas grinned sheepishly. "I come here to think, actually. I call it my thinking spot."

I'd never heard anything so adorable in my life. And I lived with a pink fairy armadillo.

"Me, too," I lied. I didn't know how else to explain my presence.

"I think he likes you," Agatha said. "And here I thought he was normal."

"Of course he's going to like *her*," Myra complained bitterly. "She's not a tree."

I did my best to ignore their running commentary so I could focus on Lucas.

"Have you been coming here since we were kids?" I asked. I found it difficult to believe this guy had escaped my notice for the past thirteen years. Then again, I did run around the island with my head up my keister most of the time, as Skye would say. I was hyper focused on achievement and little else.

"Pretty much," Lucas replied.

"Why didn't you leave the island at the first opportunity?" I asked. That was what half the high school graduates did anyway, not that I was resentful of their freedom or anything.

"I wasn't going to leave Carly behind," he said matter-of-factly. "That's my younger sister. She still had three years to go."

"What about once she graduated?"

"Her senior year, my parents announced their divorce, which was the best news Carly and I ever heard."

I laughed. "That's not what most kids say."

"They would if they had parents who fought the way ours did," Lucas said. "That's one of the main reasons I started coming here, to escape the shouting and the name calling."

"You came here...to escape?" That boy with his lightsaber that we ridiculed mercilessly had come here to escape his horrible home life. Oh, Goddess. I was a monster.

"My parents moved to different parts of the mainland as soon as Carly graduated, so we decided to stay. Carly had a serious boyfriend, and I..."

"You, what?" I asked. Oh no. Did he have a serious girlfriend?

"I didn't have anywhere I'd rather be. Without the dark

cloud of my parents hanging over me, I discovered I actually enjoyed living here. I left to train as a pilot and came straight back to take over the charter flights when Larry retired."

Larry Highland had been the main island pilot for as long as I could remember. His lush white hair and deep tan were famous among the older ladies of Eternal Springs.

"Do you and Carly still live together?" I asked.

Lucas blushed. "No, I think that would be weird at our ages. She lives with Todd, her boyfriend. The same one from high school. I have a small place on the beach, not far from the airfield."

"Sounds nice," I said.

"Ask him if there's room for you," Agatha urged.

"It's a little more isolated than where you live, but it suits me," he said.

I cringed, imagining a cramped bachelor pad with stacks of newspaper and dirty dishes scattered over the countertops.

"And you still come out to the copse to think?" I asked. "Why bother when you already live in semi-isolation?"

"A change of scenery helps me think," he said. "I like nature. The breeze that shakes the leaves. The sound of the babbling brook."

"You weren't kidding," I said. "You really do like living here."

He turned the interrogation toward me. "And you don't? You're the director of tourism. You're the island's biggest cheerleader."

I wasn't sure how to respond. "I have a complicated relationship with the island." I was telling the truth—involuntary imprisonment *was* complicated.

"But you try to make the best of it, I guess," he said.

"I do."

"That doesn't surprise me. You always struck me as having a glass half-full personality."

My brow lifted. "Really?"

"Sure. I remember when you came to the high school after your convent burned down. Most girls would've struggled to adapt to a new environment at that age. You jumped right in. By graduation, you were practically running the school." He grinned. "Not everyone appreciated your efforts, of course, but I thought you were awesome."

My heart thumped against my chest. "Awesome? Me?"

"Like some force of nature, driven by God Himself."

I frowned. "Are you religious, Lucas?"

He hesitated. "No, why? Is that a requirement for you? I guess it makes sense for a former nun-in-training."

"First of all, I was never going to be a nun, okay?"

"Okay, but..."

I pretended to zip my lip. "Never, Lucas. Second of all, a requirement for what? Why would I need you to be religious? I know plenty of people who aren't."

His head dipped between his extended arms so that I couldn't see his face. "Never mind. Forget it."

A familiar set of pale wings on a nearby branch grabbed my attention. Uh oh.

"I really need to get going," I said, rising to my feet. "I've got a lot to do before the Battle of the Bands competition." Like a murder to solve.

"You're always on the go, aren't you?" he asked. "I think this is the longest I've ever seen you stand still."

"I guess you're right about nature," I said. "It is calming." I watched out of the corner of my eye as Stuart gesticulated wildly.

"Weird. I think that white bird is having a seizure," Lucas said.

Oops. "I'll go check it out."

"You should leave it be," Lucas said. "It could have rabies."

Stuart opened his beak to protest, but I held up a quick hand to silence him. Where was Skye with a strong gust of wind when you wanted one?

I think Stuart is warning you to mind the poop, miss, Gerald said.

He saved me from stepping in it in the nick of time. I glanced down at the huge pile in front of me. "This isn't from Leia, is it?"

Don't be absurd, Agatha said. *That dog's excrement is the size of a small kitten.*

Lucas eyed the poop warily. "No. She hasn't been out here with me recently. There are a lot of cats out here, though. Could be one of them."

"That would be an awfully big cat," I said. I couldn't think of any one of them big enough to produce excrement that size. Naturally, when I wanted the trees to speak up, they remained silent. The mystery poop would have to wait for another day.

"It was nice talking to you, Lucas," I said. "I'll see you around."

"I hope so," he replied, in a tone that signified he meant it.

I pushed down the rising swarm of butterflies in my stomach. There was no time to be distracted by a hot guy. Not when there was work to be done. I'd failed once in my life and I refused to let it happen again, not ever.

Chapter Four

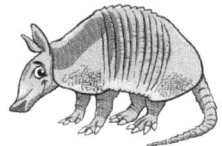

After my unsuccessful visit to the copse, I stopped by the coffee shop. I usually went in because I liked to socialize, but I had a more specific reason today. It was one of the best places to pick up gossip. If word was out about Pete's death, I'd hear about it here.

Skye must have had the same thought because, as I turned away from the counter with my blackberry tea, I ran smack into her, nearly spilling the tea in the process.

"Pete Simpson," she said, wearing a smug expression. "Drummer for Fat Gandalf. Buddy says there was a bag of weed near the body."

"The bag of pot is irrelevant. Buddy just wants to wrap this up nice and neat," I said.

"And you don't?" Skye said with a taunting cackle. "'Nice and neat' is going to be written on your tombstone. The caretaker will think you're giving him instructions."

"I want justice for Pete," I said. "Everyone deserves that."

"Justice, huh? You're getting soft in your advanced age," Skye said. "I can still remember when you blamed Obi-Wan for his own death. Said he brought it on himself. Where was your sense of justice then?" She folded her arms and glared at me.

Here we go. Skye was always ready to pick a fight. Sometimes I had the energy for it. Today, however, was not one of those days.

"I have a lot to do today, Skye," I said. "I'm sure you do, too."

"Yeah, it seems I have a murder to write about," she replied. "I guess I should start interviewing family members."

I sipped my tea, trying to remain calm. "Skye, please. Leave this alone for a bit."

Skye gorged on a cider doughnut, crumbs flying everywhere. "You said it yourself. Pete deserves justice. Freedom of the press is all about justice."

Argh. If Skye was on the case, there was no telling what kind of damage she'd cause. I had to stop her before things got out of hand, as they often did when Skye was involved.

"Give me a day or so to see what I can figure out," I pleaded quietly. "While I don't agree with Buddy that we should slap an accidental label on it and call it a day, I do need this to be kept under wraps for the sake of the town." I gave her a pointed look. "And we're well-versed in sacrificing our own desires for the sake of the town, aren't we?"

Skye licked her crumb-covered lips. Although she made an effort to appear nonchalant, I knew I had her. "Pete's brother Mike got called to the spa today for an emergency. Some electrical issue."

Perfect. He was the one I wanted to speak to first.

"Thanks for the tip, Skye. I appreciate it."

"Yeah, well. Don't get used to it."

THE TWO BROTHERS GOLF CART WAS PARKED IN THE LOT OF the Eternal Springs Spa and Resort, just as Skye said it would be. I breathed a sigh of relief. You never knew with her. It could just as easily have been a wild goose chase. Wouldn't be the first time I'd fallen for one of Skye's pranks.

I entered the familiar lobby and spotted August "Augie" Taylor, the resort's head of security. I knew Augie from the local high school, where I'd completed my senior year after the devastating fire. Even though thirteen years had passed since that night, I still vividly remembered the incident. I even suffered from nightmares on occasion. Gerald knew to turn on Mitzi's knitting show the mornings after.

"Hey, Kenna," Augie said. "What brings you here? Business or pleasure?"

The idea that I would be at the spa for pleasure was laughable. Despite the amount of time I spent here, I'd never indulged in any of the spa's offerings.

"Which do you think?" I asked.

He broke into a friendly smile. "Yeah, I figured. When are you not working?"

"When I sleep," I replied. I walked until I reached the reception counter, where Dylan Potter was checking in a guest. I waited until he'd finished before approaching the counter because I didn't want anyone to overhear our conversation.

The twenty-year-old was an easy target. He'd lived his whole life on the island and had a well-documented infatuation with the four St. Joan of Arc refugees. I often wondered what drew him to us, whether he had an untapped connection to magic or whether he was simply a horndog. I was fairly certain he didn't slobber all over himself when Winnie Jeffries was here. The buxom blonde owned Island Pizza. She made the deliveries herself in a bikini, a clever marketing ploy that showed she was smarter than people believed. Her pizza place was the only real competition for Manny's Pizza, a front for a popular bookie.

"Dylan, my love," I said effusively. "You're just the man I wanted to see."

Dylan's Adam's apple bobbed up and down. I got the impression that he was both deathly afraid of me and deathly attracted to me at the same time. It made for an interesting dynamic.

"Really? Have you changed your mind about the mud wrestling idea?" he asked hopefully.

I resisted the urge to roll my eyes. Dylan was dead set on bringing female wrestlers to compete in the famous mud pits of Eternal Springs. He was convinced it would be a huge draw for tourists and viewed it as a clever expansion of our island's brand. I disagreed with the branding argument, and I didn't want that type of tourist at any price. I had standards.

"I'm still thinking about that one, Dylan. Let me get through the Battle of the Bands first."

Dylan didn't hide his disappointment very well. "What can I do for you, then, if my idea isn't good enough?"

Oh boy. Sulking? Not attractive, Dylan.

"I'm looking for the electrician who's here," I said. "Can you tell me where he is?"

Dylan hesitated. "You know I can't give out that kind of information."

"Why? What's the problem?"

Dylan looked around cautiously before leaning closer to me across the desk. "You're not supposed to be here right now. My boss knows that a bad tourist experience reflects poorly on the whole island." Translation: Don't piss off Kenna Byrne. Fair enough. I could be prickly when I was unhappy, especially when it came to protecting the island's reputation.

"You can tell me, Dylan," I said. "I promise I won't get angry."

Dylan's eyes twinkled with possibility. "So would I be doing you a favor?"

My eyes narrowed. "No, you'd be doing your job."

Dylan cocked his head. "I think I'd be doing my job more if I don't tell you, because that's what my boss would want."

Whoa. For a gangly kid seemingly forever on the cusp of manhood, he was clever when it suited him. "Okay, Dylan. What's your price?"

"A picnic on the beach."

I tapped my nails on the desk, considering. That would actually be a romantic date if Dylan weren't at the other end of the picnic blanket. Blargh. I really wanted to speak to Mike while he was preoccupied with the job. I figured that if he had any connection to his brother's death, he'd be less able to lie if his brain and body were focused on different tasks.

"Fine. A picnic it is," I said.

Dylan seemed shocked. "Cool! All right then. Have a look in that blue day planner of yours and pick a date."

"Yes, definitely the blue one," I said. I didn't consider a picnic on the beach with Dylan Potter to be a social occasion. It was strictly business.

"Mike's in the couple's mudroom. Down the hall…"

"I know where it is, thanks." I bolted through the resort to where the couple's mudroom was located. It occurred to me as I barreled through the door that I should've asked whether there was a couple inside.

A woman's shriek alerted me to the fact that there was.

"I already complained that three's a crowd," the man grumbled. "Four is out of the question."

My attention was immediately drawn to the couple standing naked outside a Jacuzzi. Their bodies were entirely caked with the island's signature mud.

"My apologies," I said. "It's my understanding that there's an issue with the electrical system. I'm the island tourism director and it's my job to make sure this doesn't negatively impact your experience here with us."

"I'm standing outside a hot tub covered in stinky mud," the woman whined. "What kind of experience do you think we're having?"

"We were told we would go straight from the couples mud pit to the warming mineral spring tub," the man said. "When we got here, the water was ice cold."

"It's more like room temperature," a voice said. Another man sprang up from behind the hot tub.

"You must be Mike Simpson," I said. "I'm Kenna Byrne. I'm so sorry about your brother."

Mike's expression crumpled. "Thanks. Buddy said you were the one who found him. Is that true?"

I nodded mutely.

"Did he look...peaceful?"

No, he looked like he'd been murdered in the dirty men's room of a bar, but I couldn't tell him that. Mike's eyes were far too hopeful.

"He wasn't in any pain," I said truthfully. Not by the time I found him.

"I have to admit, I'm still processing the whole thing," Mike said. "He's my only sibling and I can't believe he's gone."

The mud couple exchanged glances. It was hard to read their expressions through the thick layer of sediment.

"Your brother died recently?" the man asked.

"Yesterday," Mike said.

"Yesterday?" Despite the hardened mud mask, the woman's shock was evident.

"Was he ill?" the man asked.

"No," Mike replied. "We don't exactly know what happened yet. He's my partner in the electrical company, or was. Overnight, Two Brothers has been reduced to one brother." He frowned. "I guess without a brother, I'm no brother at all." He scratched the back of his neck. "I guess I'll have to change the name."

"I wouldn't worry about the right now," I said.

"I'm really sorry," the woman said. "Here we are, making a fuss about staying covered in mud a little longer than planned, while you're working to fix it. What on earth are you doing here now? You should be home with your family, mourning your brother, not here worrying about self-absorbed spa guests like us."

Mike set down his tools. "That's kind of you to say, ma'am, but business is business. I can't afford to not answer when the resort calls. I have three kids and a wife to care for. This place is my biggest customer by a long shot. Without Pete, I'll need to work harder to keep my customers happy. It matters now more than ever."

This was my chance to ask the questions that had been on my mind.

"What if his band won the competition?" I asked. "I heard he was going to quit the company. Had he shared that with you?" I watched him closely to gauge his reaction.

"Your brother was a musician?" the mud man asked.

"Yeah, he was a drummer for a local band called Fat Gandalf," Mike said. "He'd wanted to be in a band since we were kids. It was his dream." He fixed his gaze on me. "Yeah, I knew his plan. I can't say it surprised me. He never wanted to be an electrician. He only did that to be a good brother to me. He always tried to put me first, and I let him do it." He swore under his breath.

"When did he tell you his plan?" I asked.

"We talked about it recently," Mike said. "At my son's birthday party a few weeks ago, he brought it up again."

"And you told him then that you weren't in love with the idea?"

Mike's widened. "Oh, no. I never would have said that. I

mean, we started Two Brothers together and I wanted it to stay that way, for sure. I'm not as business savvy as Pete was. We both knew how much I relied on him." He trailed off, his mouth forming a thin line.

"Did Pete care how you felt?"

"Of course! I could tell he felt guilty about it. Part of me hoped they wouldn't win the competition, so he'd have to stay on the island." Mike lowered his head. "I feel like the worst brother in the world for that now."

"Did he know you wanted him to lose?" I asked.

Mike returned his attention to the task at hand. "I would never have told him. Truthfully, I wanted him to be happy. One of us should get to live out our dream. I told him I supported him one hundred percent. He was grateful because Tiffany definitely wasn't on board with the idea."

"Tiffany's his wife?" I asked.

"Yeah," Mike said. "She made it very plain that she did not support his plan. She didn't want to follow him to the mainland for touring. She likes it here. Has a business of her own and didn't want to walk away from it."

Well, that was interesting. "Where were you yesterday morning?"

"Where I always am, on the job. I had a small refrigerator that needed to be hooked up to a new outlet at Nailed It," Mike said. "I didn't find out about Pete until I left, which was a good thing because I was able to finish that job and get paid. I ended up taking the rest of the day off. I couldn't function."

"That's understandable," I said. "It sounds like you and your brother were very close." I'd always wanted a sibling. Instead, I was saddled with my three witchy sisters from St. Joan of Arc thanks to a shared sordid history. Not exactly a bargain.

"I'm really sorry about this," Mike began, "but it looks

like I need to replace a wire here that I don't have on me. I'll have to leave and come back." He peered over the edge of the hot tub at the mud-caked couple. "I think you might have to go straight to the showers."

The couple looked at each other.

"It's not a problem," the man said. "We're relaxed, so we got the experience we came for."

"We could ask for an extra half hour with the mud blankets as compensation," the woman said, with a shrug.

They were being so gracious in light of Mike's sad circumstances that I felt inclined to do something nice. Not only that, but it would save the spa's reputation, which was obviously good for my job. As casually as I could, I brought my heat magic to my fingertips and wiggled my pinky toward the hot tub. Steam began to rise from the water.

"You fixed it!" the man exclaimed. "Looks like you don't need that wire after all."

"I think it must be your brother smiling down at you from the heavens," the woman said. "It's a mud pit miracle."

Well, my job here was done. "Enjoy your couples' time. Mike, just out of curiosity, what kind of wire did you think you needed to fix this?" Whatever it was, I'd make sure to get this hot tub fixed properly. My magic wouldn't keep it hot forever.

Mike told me as he collected his tools. "That was lucky," he said. "And believe me, I don't get to say those words very often."

"I'll walk you out," I said. "Let's leave this lovely couple to enjoy the rest of their visit alone."

Not to mention I wanted to get out of there before they immersed themselves in the water and the mud rinsed off. They were exposed enough in mud. At least there was a thick layer between their bare skin and me.

"Do you mind telling me where Tiffany lives?" I asked. "I'd like to stop by and pay my respects to her as well."

"Sure, she's over on Azalea Avenue. A green rancher with an oversized garage. That's where Pete liked to practice his drums." He smiled to himself. "I'm sure the neighbors won't miss him as much as I do."

I patted his shoulder. "I'll bet you were a really good brother, Mike."

Mike glanced at me and shrugged. "I hope so. Because he sure was one to me."

Chapter Five

I rode my scooter across town to Azalea Avenue and scanned the block for the house Mike described. As it turned out, the Simpson house was impossible to miss. I parked my scooter and stood in front of the lawn, my jaw hanging open. The yard was a minefield of pink flamingos, sunflowers, ladybugs, and other colorful metal sculptures. The largest one was a garden spinner that was at least seventy-two inches tall. When the wind hit it, the sculpture looked like rainbow confetti. The riot of colors and textures was an assault on my sense of sight. Nothing flowed. The colors weren't even complementary. It took all my resolve not to hop on my scooter and drive away.

I strode up the walkway and averted my gaze from the offending items. I rapped on the front door quickly, then slowed my pace, reminding myself that I was about to speak to Pete's widow. The woman deserved my sympathy, not my scorn...unless she was the murderer, of course. Then I would go full scorn with judgmental guns blazing.

There was no answer, but the sound of a machine drew me to the backyard. A small shed sat in the far corner of the yard, its double doors wide open. Remnants of sparks dusted the air.

"Tiffany?" I called. I didn't want to get too close and risk a stray spark singeing my clothing.

A slight blonde emerged from the shed, tipping up a protective mask. Was the band restricted to dating only blondes?

"Can I help you?" With her mask raised, I immediately noticed the dark circles under her eyes. Tiffany Simpson seemed to be sleep deprived. Whether that was from grief or guilt remained to be seen.

"Hi, Tiffany. I'm Kenna Byrne. I just wanted to come by and say how sorry I am to hear about your husband. Pete's death is a great loss to the community."

She wrinkled her nose. "Do I know you?"

"No. I'm in charge of the Battle of the Bands competition. I was there…"

Understanding spread across her pert features. "You're the woman who found him." She eyed me curiously. "What were you doing in the men's bathroom in a bar? I wanted to ask Buddy, but it seemed inappropriate given the awful news I'd just received."

To be honest, I thought it was an odd question to ask now, one day later.

"I was looking for Pete, actually," I said. "His band was ready to play, but no one could find him."

Tiffany yanked down her mask. "Yeah, well, if he hadn't been so insistent on being in that band and pursuing a music career, he might still be alive today."

Wow. She seemed far from a grieving widow. To be fair, everyone grieves differently. I know this firsthand because my witchy sisters and I had experienced four different responses in the aftermath of the destruction of St. Joan of Arc. I'd always been a hyper focused achiever, but after the incident, I sort of kicked it up a notch and never looked back. Skye had only minored in sarcasm before then, but quickly became fluent. Zola's maternal side wasn't even evident until after the fire. Up until then, she'd been happy to do her own thing. Afterward, she seemed determined to dole out sage advice and pick the nits off our backs, or would have done if we'd been gorillas. Evian became much more reliant on her familiar. Not that Paul wasn't the best toad in the world—he really is—but Evian needed to cut the cord. So maybe this tough, blasé act was Tiffany's way of coping. I didn't know her well enough to say for certain.

Tiffany retreated back into the shed and I quickly followed.

"You didn't approve of his music career?" I asked. Once I crossed the threshold, it took me a moment to get my bearings in the shed. The interior was worse than the front lawn. Disorder reigned supreme with metal sculptures everywhere I turned. Birds, flowers, a sun and stars, even a gecko. My stomach clenched and I nearly backed straight out of the shed. Then I pictured Pete's lifeless body on the floor and steeled myself against the onslaught of tacky garden decor.

"It seems you both have creative streaks," I said. I gestured to the interior of the shed. "Is that your handiwork on the front lawn, too?"

Tiffany beamed with pride. "Yes. Big Mama's Heavy Metal is the name of my company. I supply most of the shops in town with my sculptures. I'm sure you've seen them around."

Not if I'd blocked them from my memory as a matter of self-preservation.

Looking around the shed, I was surprised she didn't support her husband's interest in music.

"Was your husband a fan of your artwork?" Because I would have completely understood if he wasn't.

Tiffany began welding what appeared to be a metal ostrich. Honestly, it was hard to tell.

"Pete was very supportive of me," she said. "The problem was that Pete's creative interest clashed with mine."

"How so?" I didn't see how a drummer's dream interfered with ugly metal lawn ornaments.

She stopped welding and flipped up her mask again. "He wanted to be a full-time musician," she said hotly. "He intended to win the prize money from the competition and use it to fund his dream."

So she did know. "What's so wrong about that?"

"That meant quitting his job, spending all hours in a recording studio, and touring for months on end." She examined an imperfect piece of the ostrich. "We'd have been apart too much. It would have been bad for our marriage."

"You could have gone with him," I said.

Tiffany gaped at me as though I'd suggested removing her wisdom teeth right here and now with her welding torch. "I couldn't possibly leave all this."

Glancing around the haphazard shed, I wasn't sure how she stayed and retained her sanity.

"Did Pete know you weren't on board with his plan?" I asked.

Tiffany's expression soured. "He knew I wouldn't leave here. We fought about it more than once. He thought I'd be excited to leave Eternal Springs and travel."

I knew I would. Then again, I wasn't on the island by choice, so my attitude was bound to be colored by that simple fact.

"He seemed very confident about winning the competition," I said. "Was he always like that?"

Tiffany removed her protective gloves. "Not particularly. He did seem very confident that he'd be leaving here, though. I assumed it was wishful thinking. He'd been wanting to see the back end of Two Brothers for so long. He talked about it constantly."

"Did you think he should use the prize money for something else?" Maybe to fund the expansion of her own business?

Tiffany shrugged. "I didn't care so much about the money. I'm a girl of simple tastes. I love this house and I love what I do. Pete's the one who wanted more." Her eyes gathered unshed tears. "And now he'll never have it."

No, he wouldn't. "Were you at the practice session when he died?" I didn't recall seeing her there.

"No, I was at Marta's Vineyard discussing supplies. She wants more bee ornaments in the next delivery. They apparently sell well to the beekeeper crowd."

There was a beekeeper crowd on the island? That was news to me.

"You can never have enough bee ornaments," I lied enthusiastically. I knew Marta Hammond, so Tiffany's story would be easy enough to check out.

Tiffany regarded me. "You know what? If you're the tourism director, maybe you could find a way to get my sculptures into more local shops. That Gigi Montbatten refuses to stock my stuff. Like she's too classy for pink flamingos. It's insulting."

Gigi Montbatten owned A Touch of Elegance gift shop. I could hardly blame her for rejecting the menagerie of metal monstrosities.

"I'll see what I can do," I said. "Again, I'm sorry for your loss."

Tiffany pulled down her protective mask, ready to get back to work. Burying oneself in work was a sentiment I understood all too well.

. . .

I'd traveled only a block from Tiffany's house when I spotted it—the Waffle Wagon. The red wagon was at the far end of Thistledown Road, preparing to make a right turn. If I put the pedal to the metal, I might be able to catch up before I lost sight of it. As I was about to make a move, a splotch of black and white on the side of the road ahead caught my eye. My hands gripped the handlebar as I felt my blood pressure rise. Once again, the Waffle Wagon would have to wait.

I pulled over and whipped off my helmet. "Clover!" I yelled. "What do you think you're doing? We've talked about this."

Zola's skunk familiar was notorious for playing dead in order to fool tourists. She'd lure innocent passersby to the side of the road like a stinky siren, and then hop to her feet, delighting the tourists with her miraculous recovery. In return, they'd ply her with treats.

"How many times have I told you it's not okay to play roadkill?" I demanded, my hands flying to my hips.

Clover ignored me, which only made my blood boil more.

"Answer me, Clover, or I will drown you in lava." Okay, that threat was a bit extreme, I admit, but I was pissed.

It was then that I noticed the blood.

I took a hesitant step forward. "Clover?"

"Kenna, I'm so glad you're here." Stuart swooped down from nowhere and I swatted him back.

"Not now, Stuart," I said, scooping up Clover and placing her in the basket of my scooter. I had to get her to Zola's for immediate help. The skunk was unconscious, and I couldn't find the source of the bleeding. This was the ultimate case of the skunk that cried wolf.

"But I saw what happened," Stuart insisted, flying beside me.

I strapped on my helmet and fired up the scooter. "I can

guess what happened. Clover's roadkill game almost became a reality." I headed toward Cackleberries, Zola's garden shop.

As usual, Stuart continued rambling. The albino raven could never take a hint, no matter how strongly worded. Thanks to the helmet and the wind whipping around my ears, all I heard was garbled ravenspeak.

"I need to get to Zola right now," I shouted. "I'll talk to you later."

I made it to Cackleberries in less than five minutes. I lifted Clover into my arms and rushed inside, the door slamming behind me before Stuart had a chance to follow. Zola was behind the counter, crushing herbs in a mortar with a pestle.

"What happened?" she asked, alarmed.

"Not sure. I found her on the side of the road. She must've actually gotten hit by a golf cart or a scooter."

Zola's expression darkened. "And left for dead? Who would do such a thing? Bring her to the back."

I hurried behind her to the back of the shop and gently placed Clover on a wooden table.

Zola set to work gathering ingredients to concoct a healing tonic for her familiar. As the earth witch of our foursome, she was the most adept at plant-based magic—something that came in handy during times like this.

"I don't think she was hit by a scooter," Zola said, as she began to treat Clover's injuries.

"Why not?" I leaned over to examine the skunk.

"The wounds don't match what I'd expect from impact with a vehicle," Zola said. "She's battered and bruised, but the injuries aren't consistent with being hit by a scooter or a golf cart."

A tapping on the back window caused us both to jump.

"Stuart!" I yelled. "Not now."

"Seriously? Is that albino raven still hounding you?" Zola queried. "Can't you get a restraining order?"

"He's trying to pull an *All About Eve* and replace Gerald as my familiar," I said.

"What does he think is so great about being your familiar?" Zola asked, her eyes riveted to Clover as she worked her magic on the skunk's limp body.

"He has good taste," I said. "Other than that, I really don't know. He thinks it's his true calling."

"Gerald is an absolute treasure," Zola said. "Does Stuart realize how versatile that armadillo is? Those are hard wings to fill."

Stuart continued tapping on the window.

"I can't concentrate with that racket," Zola said. "Make your stalker go away."

I went and opened the back door. "Get a move on, Stuart. We're trying to focus on helping Clover."

"Flying monkeys attacked Clover," Stuart said quickly, before I had a chance to close the door.

My hand hovered over the doorknob. "What?"

"Flying monkeys," he repeated.

"There's no such thing," I replied.

The words tumbled out in a rush. "I saw them. Three of them. Big and ugly. They flew down and attacked Clover."

"Are you sure they weren't birds?"

Stuart's beady eye fixed on me. "I'm a raven, Kenna. Do you think I wouldn't recognize another bird?"

Flying monkeys? How was that even possible? "You're saying they attacked Clover and then flew off?"

Stuart nodded. "Back toward the forest."

That explained the strange poop in the Cottonmouth Copse.

"Okay, Stuart. Thanks for the intel." If there were flying monkeys about, I had a sinking feeling I knew where they were coming from. Great Goddess of Mercy, I did *not* need this right now.

"So you'll promote me now?" he asked eagerly.

"It doesn't work that way and you know it," I said. "But I do appreciate the tip." I closed the door before he could object.

When I returned to the table, Zola was feeding Clover from a baby bottle. I heaved a sigh of relief.

"You literally baby your familiar," I said.

Zola patted the skunk's head. "She was nearly killed. Show some compassion."

"I rescued her, didn't I?"

Zola's expression softened. "You did. Thank you." She stroked the skunk's soft fur as she worked in more of the tonic. "Flying monkeys, huh?"

"Seems so."

Zola's jaw tensed. "Well, that's the reason we're here. The cleanup crew."

I nodded. "I'll take care of it."

Zola's eyes met mine. "Are you sure? I feel like you're already so busy."

"We're all busy, Zola. If I need help, I'll let you know."

Zola smoothed Clover's fur. "I wish that fire had never happened."

"Preaching to the converted, Zola."

"Where did you find her?" she asked, frowning.

"I was leaving Azalea Avenue and headed toward...the Waffle Wagon," I admitted.

Zola suppressed a laugh. "You're still chasing waffles?"

"They're not just any waffles," I said. "They're liege Belgian waffles. They're made differently from other waffles."

"With all your island connections, you'd think you could track down the Waffle Wagon," Zola said with an amused shake of her head. "What were you doing on Azalea Avenue? That's not your neighborhood."

"Talking to Pete Simpson's wife," I replied.

Zola cocked her auburn head. "Who's Pete Simpson?"

"The dead drummer from Fat Gandalf."

"Oh, I heard about that from Skye." She shot me a quizzical look. "Wait, aren't you the one that found him?"

I nodded. "In the men's room at Anchors Away."

She squinted. "What were you doing in the men's room?"

A common question today. "Looking for Pete. Practice was about to start and no one could find him. Speaking of which, you'll come to the competition, won't you? I could use the support."

"Battle of the Bands?" Zola asked with a grimace. "You know all that commotion isn't my jam."

"There'll be rum runners," I promised.

When Zola chewed her lip, I knew I had her. "Which day is it again?"

"Next Saturday," I replied. Clover stirred and her eyes fluttered open. "She'll be okay now, won't she?"

Yes. Thank you, Clover said.

"Did you see the flying monkeys, Clover?" Zola asked.

Clover froze with fear. *Three of them*. She shuddered before fainting.

"Poor Clover," Zola said, and pressed her ear to her familiar's chest. "The tonic will work, but she needs rest." Her brow creased. "If there are actual flying monkeys loose on the island...I'm worried about the cats."

The island has a healthy population of stray cats that lived in the forest due to the evacuation of the coven thirteen years ago. A group of familiars refused to budge from the island, despite their mistresses' pleas. They ended up staying behind like the four of us and reproducing at the rate you'd expect for stray cats.

"I'll make sure they're okay," I promised.

"Even Tut?" Zola asked. The annoying hairless cat acted as the de facto leader of the stray cat faction.

There'd been enough death in Eternal Springs for one week. I didn't need a trio of flying monkeys to add to the body count. Not on my watch.

I straightened my shoulders. "Even Tut," I agreed.

Chapter Six

Despite Pete's death and the flying monkey issue, I had to focus on the competition. This event was my baby, and I had to make sure everything was in place for the Battle of the Bands to succeed. If the event was a flop, Buddy might not fund another of my ideas ever again. He could even—gulp—have me fired. This was my big attempt to expand the reputation of Eternal Springs to include music and I needed to promote it like crazy. The key to promotion on the island meant one thing--HEX 66.6.

I pushed open the door to the office of the island radio station, owned by my witchy sister, Evian. Most of the time, I resisted the urge to ask for favors because I hated owing any of that trio. Inevitably, I regretted their involvement in any of my tourist-related activities. Or my life, for that matter.

"If it isn't Firestarter," Evian announced to nobody. "What Eternal Springs event brings you here?" She held up a finger. "Oh, wait. Let me guess. Starts with 'battle' and ends with 'bands.'"

"I resent the implication that I only come to you on official business," I said.

Evian brightened. "You mean you're not here with your tourism hat on?"

"Oh, I definitely am," I said, and felt a pang of guilt when I noticed her crestfallen expression. "I need as much coverage of the competition as you can offer. From the time it starts in the morning, until the winners are announced that night."

Evian consulted her schedule. "I blocked off from nine to nine."

"No, that's not enough," I pleaded. "You'll need to be there far later than nine to include coverage of the winners."

"I've been playing songs by the participants all week," Evian said. "Thanks for that list, by the way."

"You're welcome. There's going to be a lot of talent in one place," I said.

"What about Skye?" Evian asked. "Will she be covering it for The Town Croaker?"

"Of course, but that won't print until the next day," I said. "I want the music to be piped into every establishment on the island possible. The only way to do that is through the radio station."

"It'll be a nice break from '80s music," Evian said. She inclined her head. "The bands won't play '80s music, will they?"

"They're not cover bands," I said. "They play original songs."

Evian wiped her brow. "Phew. Thank Goddess for that small mercy." She marked her schedule with a red pen. "Fine. I'll continue live coverage for as long as you like."

I tensed. "Really? What's the catch?"

Evian smiled. "What makes you think there's a catch?"

"Because I've known you far longer than I'd like to."

"That's a bit mean." She pretended to sulk.

"Where's Paul?" I asked, craning my neck to see around

her desk. Sometimes Evian brought him to work with her. I tended to leave Gerald at home to take care of domestic duties.

"He wanted to hop over to the pond today," Evian said. "Do a little sunbathing. I was tempted to say no, but I'm trying to support his independence."

"The pond in the woods?" I queried.

Her brow furrowed. "That's his usual hangout. Why?"

After what happened to Clover, I figured I'd better warn her about the flying monkey problem. Ugh. I hated to say this when she was finally making an effort to extend Paul's leash.

"You should have him steer clear of that area for the time being," I said. "Have him stick close to home."

"Why? You're one of the people harping that Paul needs a break from me every now and again. And he values his 'me time.'"

"He also values his life." I shared what happened to Clover, and Evian gasped.

"They have to be coming from that hellhole," she insisted.

"That's the running theory," I replied. "I'm going to set them on the highway back to hell as soon as I'm able."

"I'm glad Clover's going to be okay," Evian said.

"Me, too, but maybe she'll finally learn a lesson and stop playing dead," I grumbled.

Evian suppressed a smile. "You really hate that, don't you?"

I didn't respond. "Do you remember Skywalker?"

Evian burst into laughter. "How could I forget that sweet boy battling branches with a lightsaber? He was amazing!"

"He's even more amazing now," I blurted out before I could stop myself.

Evian arched an eyebrow. "Is that so? Do tell."

I was stuck now. I'd raised the topic, after all. What did I expect to happen?

"I just mean he's very successful. He's a pilot."

She studied me. "How is that successful in your eyes? You hate the idea of flying. You flunked Broomstick 101 because you refused to leave the ground."

"And it destroyed my GPA, too," I said hotly. That fact still rankled me.

"He still goes to the Cottonmouth Copse," I said. "It's his thinking spot."

"Does he pack any heat?" She laughed at her own joke. "And, by that, I mean his lightsaber."

"No, but he sometimes brings his Great Dane, Leia."

She laughed again, clutching her stomach. "His dog is named after Princess Leia? Classic."

"He seems incredibly nice," I said. "I feel bad about what we did to him."

Evian shrugged. "Look, those kids weren't exactly welcoming to us when we left St. Joan's."

"But Lucas wasn't one of them," I objected. "We only pranked him because the opportunity presented itself, not because he deserved it."

Evian fiddled with the pen on her desk. "I guess that's true. Well, what do you want to do about it now? We can't go back in time."

"Nothing," I said. "I'm feeling guilty, that's all."

"There's something new," Evian said.

I shot her a quizzical look. "Why the sarcasm?"

"No reason."

I pressed my palms flat on her desk. "There's obviously a reason or you wouldn't have said it."

Evian put her fingers to her lips and turned an invisible key, then tossed it over her shoulder.

"Your vault is weak," I said. "I can get it out of you if I really want to."

"Then maybe I'll reconsider our arrangement for the

Battle of the Bands." Evian offered a smile of sugary sweetness. "Goodness me, Kenna, are those tears? But you're usually so reserved."

Water splashed onto my cheeks and I touched the so-called tears. "Very funny, Evian."

"Reducing yourself to waterworks to get your way. Really now, Kenna." She clucked her tongue. "I would have thought such behavior was beneath you."

"There's going to be a pit of lava beneath you in about two seconds if you don't back off," I warned.

"You have such violent tendencies," Evian said. "Has anyone ever told you that?"

"You're just jealous because your best move involves wet pants."

Evian twirled her finger in the air. "It can be awfully embarrassing, especially for a neat-freak like yourself."

The twirling finger was my cue to leave. "This conversation isn't over, Aquawitch."

"It is for now." She wiggled her fingers at me. "Toodles."

I LEFT THE RADIO STATION IN A HUFF. MY WITCHY SISTERS had a way of getting under my skin like no others. Why was Evian under the impression that I suffered from some kind of post-traumatic guilt? I mean, we were all scarred by the Incident. I wasn't any worse than the other three.

Standing on the pavement, I realized that Marta's Vineyard was at the far end of the block, on the corner. There was no time like the present to confirm Tiffany's story.

Marta Hammond was a stout woman with wiry hair, usually pulled up in a severe bun. Her hair was the color I dreaded—not the sleek silver some women were blessed with as they matured, but the dull, lifeless gray that reeked of old age and decay.

"Kenna, what a nice surprise," Marta said. She stood in the birdhouse aisle, swapping out price stickers.

"Hi, Marta," I said. "How's business?"

"Not too bad," she said. "It's cyclical, like most businesses. What brings you by? Something for your garden?" She paused. "I tried to order you a custom armadillo lawn ornament, but no one seems to make them."

"Can't say I'm surprised," I shrugged, "but I appreciate the thought." And I was grateful for their non-existence. The last thing I wanted was a metal armadillo on my front lawn. My garden was perfectly symmetrical. A lawn ornament on one side would unbalance the landscape.

"How's everything going?" Marta asked. "I don't suppose you've snagged yourself a serious boyfriend yet."

Marta seemed to think every woman's goal in life should be marriage, quickly followed by children. One some level, it was amazing that she ran her own shop. Then again, she only started the shop after her husband left her for another man. Hal Hammond was one of those men who seemed obviously gay to everyone except Hal and Marta. It was only when famed performance artist Rodrigo Gomez came to the island to perform in the mud pits that Hal experienced his sexual awakening. Hal quickly swapped his overalls for skinny jeans and his wife for Rodrigo. The happy couple moved to the mainland five years ago to escape the scrutiny that followed. Despite Marta's experience, she still seemed to adhere to a certain belief system that tied a woman's success in life to her marital status.

"I'm too busy to worry about that," I said vaguely.

"I have plenty of attractive young men shopping in here," Marta said. "I'd be happy to set you up."

"Save them for yourself," I replied.

She chuckled. "They're far too young for me. I'm lucky if I can attract the attention of the gentlemen at the senior center. Even the eighty-year-olds want to date fifty-year-olds. That puts me out of the running."

I felt a pang of sympathy for Marta. It couldn't have been easy, dealing with Hal's abandonment under the watchful gaze of the whole town. Five years later and Hal was still in wedded bliss with Rodrigo, while Marta toiled away amongst birdhouses and pink flamingo ornaments.

"I have a fulfilling life," I said. "I love my job and I have the best armadillo a person could ever hope for."

Marta set down her pricing gun. "I hope you don't mind me asking, but do you still think of yourself as married to God? Because maybe that's the problem."

I bristled. "There's no problem, Marta, and I do not think of myself as married to God." The convent had been the coven's cover story for St. Joan of Arc, a cover story I bitterly regretted as an adult woman still stuck in Eternal Springs. I felt like I'd never shake the reputation loose. Maybe that was half the reason no guys ever asked me out.

"You know, if you're saving yourself for marriage, there are plenty of things you can still do…"

I cut her off immediately "Marta, as it happens, I'm not religious, but thank you for the tutorial."

Marta pursed her lips. "I guess that's the result of the fire, huh? Did you feel like God punished you and your friends?"

Murder investigation or not, I was beginning to regret stopping in here.

"I prefer not to talk about that time in my life," I snapped. That much was true. While I couldn't put physical distance between the island and me, I could put emotional distance between the Incident and me.

"Perfectly understandable," Marta said. "A terrible shame about that dead saxophonist, isn't it?" Marta gave a sad shake of her head.

"Dead saxophonist?" I said.

She blinked in confusion. "Aren't you the one who found him?"

"Oh, you mean Pete." I actually felt relieved. For a split second, I thought the island had another musical victim. "He was a drummer."

Marta slapped another price on a birdhouse. "Drug overdoses are such a tragic waste of a life."

I felt my blood pressure begin to rise. "Who said it was a drug overdose?"

"He took too much pot," she said matter-of-factly. "He was trying to boost his energy level for his performance."

I smacked my forehead. Did I need to educate this woman on marijuana? Because I really didn't want that job.

"The toxicology report hasn't come back yet," I said. "And pot...You can't..." I shook it off and focused on the reason I was here. "I understand you were with Pete's wife when he died."

Marta appeared surprised. "Was I?"

"She said she was here discussing a delivery with you that morning," I pressed.

Marta kneaded her earlobe, thinking. "Which morning was it? Tiffany was here recently. I remember we talked about more bee ornaments."

That made sense in conjunction with Tiffany's statement. "It would have been Tuesday. Does that sound right to you?"

Marta's eyes lit up. "Yes, yes, it does. After she left, I had an appointment with my podiatrist to deal with my bunions. That was Tuesday."

The bell over the front door jingled as someone else entered the shop.

"What have we here?" Buddy ambled into the shop, assisted by Mitzi. She looked like she was about to collapse under the strain of his ample weight. "Kenna, I hope you're here to talk Marta into coming to the Battle of the Bands."

"But who would mind my shop?" Marta asked.

I took the opportunity to pump Buddy for information. "Have the results of the toxicology report on Pete Simpson come in?"

"Um, not yet," Buddy said, in a way that suggested there was a snafu with the report. "These things take time, but I have no doubt drugs are the culprit." He said the last part loudly, as though other people were in the shop who needed to overhear.

"Mitzi, I really enjoyed this week's show," I said. The woman had to have a rough life, sleeping next to Buddy every night. I figured I'd throw her a bone.

Mitzi cheered slightly. "Thanks, I didn't know you were a fan."

"I listen all the time," I said. "It's very soothing." Like anesthesia.

"Listen, Kenna," Buddy said. "I'm not sure why you're hanging around Marta's Vineyard when you should be out there making me...I mean, Eternal Springs look good." He was doing that thing when he tries to sound charming, but ends up sounding like a pompous ass. In other words, he spoke.

Marta interjected, "She was asking me about..."

"Lawn ornaments," I said. "I've been thinking about adding a splash of color to my yard." I didn't want Buddy to know I was skulking around town asking questions about Pete. He'd accuse me of undermining his authority, which I kind of was.

"Good thinking," Buddy said. "The house is a nice shade of purple, but everything else is white and black. You could spruce it up with some orange or green."

I fought the urge to gag. Instead, I forced an enthusiastic smile. "Thanks for the idea. I'll take it under advisement." I turned to Marta. "It was great to see you. I need to get a move on or my schedule will completely fall apart."

Buddy wagged a finger at me. "As long as your big event doesn't completely fall apart. I'm counting on you, Kenna Byrne. You know what happens to people who let me down."

You eat them? I wanted to ask. "Failure isn't in my wheelhouse, Buddy."

At least I hoped not, or there was a lot more at stake than a music competition.

Chapter Seven

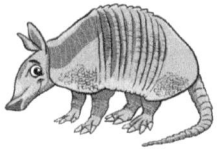

I trudged up the front porch steps and unlocked the door. Although the day was only partially over, I felt ready to crawl into bed and pull the covers over my head. Naps weren't in my nature, but sleep looked very appealing right now. I attempted to open the door, but it only budged an inch. What the hellmouth? I peered inside the house to see what was blocking the door and realized that it was my couch.

"Gerald," I yelled. "Why is my couch blocking the door?"

I am frightfully sorry, miss, Gerald said. *Not to worry. I'm working on a solution right now.*

"A solution for what?" All I wanted to do was get into my house and relax, listen to a little Mitzi on the radio, and release the stress of the day.

I think it would be best if you waited to come inside, Gerald said. *Perhaps you could go down to the coffee shop for a bit. Head to the beach or perhaps visit a friend?*

"Visit a friend?" I queried. "Gerald, let me in right now." I didn't wait for him to respond. Instead, I pushed the door as hard as I could until there was a gap large enough for me to climb over the couch. I stood in my living room, gobsmacked.

"What in the Goddess's name...?" The furniture looked as if it had been arranged by a toddler group. The contents of the kitchen cabinets seemed to have found a new home on my living room floor. Things were...messy. My throat was too dry to speak.

I warned you, miss. Gerald appeared from upstairs. *This won't be good for your mental state.*

My eyes bulged. "You think?" Everywhere I turned was a punch in the boob. Every single thing appeared to be out of place. "Are you trying to kill me?"

Quite the opposite, Gerald said. *I was researching an organizational spell, one designed to kick in automatically whenever something is out of order and make it right.*

"Let me guess," I said. "You suffered a setback."

It's merely a glitch, Gerald said. *I'm quite sure I can mend it, but I need time. I was not expecting you home so early or I would have held off on the experiment.*

I struggled to control my breathing. I felt an anxiety attack coming on if I didn't get out of here soon. "Does the whole house look this bad?"

I would advise you not to go upstairs, miss. It's much worse.

"Worse?" I shouted. How could it be worse than what I was seeing down here? I couldn't bear the thought.

Please go for now, Gerald said. *I can assure you I'll have this back to your usual high standards before teatime.*

"You'd better," I said, pointing a finger at him, "because Stuart is looking pretty good to me right now."

From outside the living room window, I heard a muffled cry of joy.

I pulled the sofa away from the door so that I could escape. I didn't want to say anything to Gerald that I'd regret.

I went to climb on my scooter and immediately noticed

its condition had changed. Although I'd left it only for a few minutes, Zola had managed to get to it. I guess my help with Clover wasn't enough to stave off her retribution. The entire scooter was covered in the island's famous mud. Leave it to the earth witch to use mud in her prank. I knew why she'd done it, but her timing couldn't have been worse. I was already apoplectic about my house. This was not helping my mood.

"Incoming," Stewart called. "Out of the way."

Instinctively, I took a step back. It was a good thing, too, because Stuart swooped down with a bucket clenched in his beak. He tipped the bucket over the scooter and dumped scratch doused it with water. It wasn't enough to remove all the mud, but it was a good start.

"Thanks, Stuart," I said. "That's very proactive of you."

"If you want to take a walk, I'll have this cleaned off for you by the time you get back," Stuart said.

"You don't have to do that," I said. "It's not your job." Then again, I didn't want to spend the rest of the afternoon scrubbing my scooter clean. It was too close to the mess that was inside my house. I needed to put some distance between chaos and me. Chaos was my Kryptonite.

"That's very kind of you," I said. "I think I'll take your suggestion and walk into town. My heart could use the exercise." And I knew exactly where I wanted to go.

"I'll be here," Stuart called after me. "Getting the job done for you!"

I walked into town, slowing my pace when I reached Cackleberries. Zola wouldn't expect me to show up so soon. She probably expected me to still be obsessing over the mess.

When I entered the shop, her expression of shock confirmed my theory.

"Kenna," she said. "How did you get here?"

"Not on my scooter," I said, "but I'm sure you already know that."

Zola couldn't disguise her guilty expression. "It was only payback for the candle wax."

"You do realize that I wasn't responsible for that prank, don't you?" Apparently not.

Zola stared at me for a long moment before understanding rippled across her features. "It was Skye, wasn't it?"

I nodded. "She was messing with me by messing with you." I should have cleared up the confusion when it happened, but I was so busy with work that I didn't want to spend the time correcting Skye's childish behavior. Lesson learned.

"I'm really sorry, Kenna," Zola said. "I should have realized it wasn't your style."

No, it certainly wasn't. Skye had replaced Zola's hair removal wax with candle wax that smelled like honey. When Zola went outside into her garden, her legs were attacked by a swarm of bees. And judging by the slight swelling still evident on her face, the bees got to her upper lip, as well. Thankfully, as an earth witch, she was able to subdue the bees before too much damage was done.

"The wax still managed to remove the hair," Zola said. "I'm still trying to figure that one out."

"You also should have realized that I would never deal in melted wax," I said. "Just because I specialize in flames doesn't mean I'd let things get out of hand." Everyone knew I disliked mess and disorder.

"You even like all your wicks to be the same length," Zola said, shaking her head. "How could I be so foolish?"

"Don't feel bad," I said. "Skye designed the prank so that we would both suffer. She knew your reprisal would involve dirt."

"We need to pay her back for this," Zola said.

I waved my hands frantically. "No more," I said. "It will only escalate matters. I don't have time to deal with anymore nonsense."

"Well, I owe you one," Zola said. "Is there anything you need from the shop? I won't charge you."

I scanned the array of jars and vials. "What I could really use right now are cackleberries. How are you fixed for those?"

Zola groaned. "Anything else, I could give you in a heartbeat. You know how precious cackleberries are, though."

I did know. I also knew the Cottonmouth Copse had been cleaned out by Skye.

"Do you have anything else that could serve as a substitute?" I asked.

Zola studied me. "Why? Do you need truth serum? I have no doubt that Skye will cop to this latest prank. I'm sure she's proud of herself."

"It isn't for Skye," I said. "I want to have it in case I need to grill a suspect about Pete's murder."

"You're grilling suspects now? I thought you were dealing with the flying monkeys."

"I can multitask. You know that."

"I heard Pete's death was a drug overdose," Zola said. She crushed a planet of berries and dumped them into a blender.

"That's Buddy talking," I said. "You know him. He wants this to be cut and dry."

Zola tossed in a handful of flower petals and pressed the button. "But you don't agree?"

"I don't," I said. Although life would be easier if I did. "I can't afford to have a murderer running around town. What if someone's targeting musicians?"

Zola's brow creased. "Like a serial killer? Could it have been the monkeys?"

"You think flying monkeys invaded the men's bathroom at Anchors Away, killed a man by knocking his head against the toilet seat, and then flew away without anyone noticing?"

Zola chewed her lip. "Well, when you put it that way…"

"So far, I've ruled out Pete's wife and his brother," I said. "Those are the two people closest to him. So what if it wasn't personal? What if it was someone who wants to knock off the competition? Fat Gandalf is favored to win the competition." For a brief moment, I wondered how Pete's death affected the odds.

"I don't know how you keep so many plates spinning at once, Kenna," Zola said. "I'm perfectly happy here in Cackleberries, doing my thing."

"Maybe that attitude is the reason we're stuck here," I said.

Zola's head snapped toward me. "Are you serious? You're going to bring that up now? I just complimented you!"

"It's true," I said. "If we'd been more alert, instead of 'doing our own thing,' as you put it, maybe the Incident That Shall Not Be Named never would have happened. We'd be living our lives in a place of our own choosing, instead of stuck here like genies in a bottle, chasing after flying monkeys."

Zola gaped at me. "Now I'm glad I don't have any cackleberries. And, even if I did, I wouldn't give them to you."

"You don't need them to make truth serum for *me*, Zola," I said. "I'll always tell you what's on my mind."

Her expression clouded over. "That may be true, but maybe some things are better left unsaid."

I left Cackleberries feeling worse than when I'd arrived. At least when I got there, I was energized by anger. Now I simply felt guilty for what I'd said to Zola. It wasn't her laid-back style that caused the incident at St. Joan of Arc.

She didn't deserve my ire. Part of me wanted to go back and apologize, but my pride kept me from doing so. Another time, when I felt calmer and more in control.

I took a few cleansing breaths and continued walking through town. Something I thought to myself in Cackleberries was sticking with me. *How did Pete's death affect the odds?* What if my theory was right? What if Pete's murder had something to do with the competition and nothing to do with his personal life? I had no doubt that people would be betting on the outcome. There were three prizes to be won—first, second, and third place. Whenever there was a winner to be announced, there was sure to be gambling behind the scenes. And I happened to know one of the primary bookies in town. Although gambling isn't legal in Eternal Springs, Buddy turned a blind eye, mostly because he liked to place bets, too. Before I could stop myself, I headed straight to Manny's Pizza.

I bypassed the counter when I arrived, and left the acne-riddled teenager staring after me. He was clearly torn between his need to stop me and his fear of me. No doubt my hardened expression was enough to keep anyone at bay, even Manny Alfredo's nephew.

The door to his office was open, so I sauntered in. "How's it going, Manny?"

He glanced up from his heaping plate of chicken parm with a side of spaghetti. He wore a red and white-checkered handkerchief around his neck. "Kenna Byrne, if it isn't my favorite director of tourism. Have a seat, sweetheart. You hungry? I can ask Johnnie for another plate."

"Not hungry, but thank you," I said. I never eat spaghetti. I can't stand the way the noodles splashed sauce everywhere and constantly slipped off the fork. I preferred penne pasta that I can easily stab without incident.

"To what do I owe the pleasure of your attractive

company?" Manny asked, dabbing the corners of his mouth with the handkerchief. There was still a spot of sauce on the tip of his nose, and I was sorely tempted to wipe it off myself. I couldn't seem to focus on anything except the red splotch.

"I was wondering if you were planning to attend the Battle of the Bands competition," I said. "It's obviously in the town's interest to have a full house."

"Of course," he said. "I wouldn't dream of missing a major event like that. I fully support our splendid community here, you know that."

I smiled. "Good. By any chance, are you engaged in any side activities related to the competition?"

He flashed a look of mock indignation. "My dear Kenna. What are you suggesting?"

I tapped my fingers on the arms of the chair. "Listen, Manny. I'm not here to get you in trouble. I'm just curious if anyone has big money riding on Fat Gandalf tanking in the competition."

He removed the handkerchief and set it on the desk. "Of course I do. Fat Gandalf is the favorite. It's inevitable somebody would bet against them."

"Who has the biggest stake?" I asked.

Manny sucked down Mountain Dew through a giant green crazy straw. With his big brown eyes and chubby cheeks, he looked oddly adorable. "You know I can't reveal confidential information about my clientele."

"The person's not going to get in trouble for betting, I promise." I couldn't promise they wouldn't get in trouble for murder, though. That would be out of my hands.

"Kenna, you know I have a soft spot for pale skin and freckles—it's like you were carved from a bar of Irish Spring soap—but some things are simply not done, and this is one of them."

I wracked my brain to think of something Manny could want. "What if I made it worth your while?"

He steepled his thick fingers. "Miss Byrne, are you trying to make me an offer I can't refuse?"

"Not exactly." Just an offer that he would really, really want to accept. "How about a free pass to the mud pits for the rest of the year? Think of how amazing your skin will look. The mud is far more magical than Irish Spring."

He examined his hairy arms. "I like my skin fine the way it is." His brow furrowed. "You think my skin needs help? Like it doesn't glow enough already?"

Uh oh. The last thing I wanted was to insult Manny Alfredo. "No, not at all. Your skin is—" I caught myself before I said apelike. "It has the elasticity of a twenty year old."

"Not a twenty-year-old like Johnnie, I hope," he said. "That kid still has acne in more places than I care to look."

My gaze fixed on his chewed fingernails. He wore rings on almost every finger, probably in an effort to distract from his unattractive habit.

"How about a weekly appointment with Sara at Nailed It? She does the best manicures in town. I swear by her." I held up my hands for him to view my perfectly manicured nails.

Manny's interest appeared piqued. "They look good. For the rest of the year, you say?"

"Absolutely," I said. "Sara is very accommodating. I'll make sure she fits you into her schedule." If there was one thing I could handle, it was scheduling.

Manny stared at his nails. "I've tried everything to stop biting them. Nothing works. Maybe if I have a weekly manicure, that will keep them too nice and tidy to chew."

I gave him a reassuring smile. "Sounds like a good plan. So what do you say?"

Manny leaned forward. "The guy you wanna to talk to is Seymour Fraser."

"Seymour? As in Segue Seymour?"

Manny splayed his hands. "I'm a man of my word. I can't help it if you don't like the answer."

"No, that's fine. It's just not a name I expected to hear. Thanks. I'll let Sara know you'll be in touch."

"Remember. You didn't get his name from me," Manny said.

"Got it...or, no, I didn't get it. From you, that is."

"Good girl." He paused. "What about pedicures? Will she do those, too?" He held up a sandal-clad foot.

Manny Alfredo wore leather sandals? How had I never noticed that before? Good grief. His toenails looked as shabby as his fingernails. I didn't want to contemplate how that happened. Gross.

"I'd be happy to sort that out for you, Manny," I said. I considered it a public service. Nobody should be subjected to those feet. Nobody.

"Thanks, Kenna," he replied. "You're a peach."

Chapter Eight

Every town has its own "weird guy" and Seymour Fraser was ours. He wore his hair in a buzz cut except for a few longer strands in the front, which were dyed orange. With his long, pointy nose and his beady eyes, he resembled the exotic birds that he sold at his shop, Feathered Friends. It didn't help that he wore brightly colored suits. And did I mention he rode around town on a Segue? There were times I passed him on the road when he looked downright sinister. He was like a Bond villain without the cool evil lair.

Birds squawked loudly as I entered the shop. Appropriately enough, a Flock of Seagulls' song played through the speakers. It was difficult to hear, with the incessant shrieking of the birds in the background, but I know my '80s music.

Seymour parted the beaded curtain behind the counter and gazed at me curiously. "You're not here for a bird, are you?"

I feigned interest in the nearest cage that hung from the ceiling. "I don't know. This one is awfully pretty."

"Pretty?" Seymour balked. "He's *gorgeous*. A rare gem in the bird world."

"I like rare gems."

Seymour folded his arms petulantly. "I'm afraid he's not for sale."

I blinked. "How is he not for sale? There's a price tag right here." I flicked the piece of paper tied to the cage with a string of red ribbon.

"That price is for the cage, not the bird," Seymour said.

I scanned the tag. "It very clearly states that the price is for the bird. Cage sold separately." I whirled around. "Why don't you want me to have a bird?" Now that he'd told me I couldn't, I really wanted one.

"You're just not the right kind of owner," he said vaguely.

I recoiled. "Are you kidding? I'm the best owner possible. I'm neat. I'm clean. I work on a consistent schedule, so the bird would never miss a meal." Gerald would make sure of it.

Seymour shook his head, his orange strands of hair tangled in his long eyelashes. He blew the hair away with a single breath. "Nope. Sorry. I reserve the right to reject buyers. My shop, my rules."

I was flabbergasted. No one had ever deemed me unfit before, not since the Incident.

"I'm wonderful with animals," I said.

"With one animal," Seymour countered. "Singular. A pink fairy armadillo, if I'm not mistaken."

I narrowed my eyes. "How do you know that?"

He swished his hand in the air. "I pay attention, Miss Byrne. It's what I do." He cocked his head in the attentive of style of the birds that surrounded me.

Alrighty then. "It's your loss, little guy." I peered into the cage and noticed the paper lining the bottom of the cage. "Hey, is that my quarterly newsletter?" Goddess above, it *was*.

Seymour had the good sense to look apologetic. "I have to

line the cages with *something*. I always know where I can gather discarded newsletters."

I tried to focus on the reason for my visit, because that matter was more pressing than my fragile ego. "So are you excited about the Battle of the Bands competition?"

Seymour pulled a bag of seeds from behind the counter and walked to one of the bird cages. He placed a seed on the tip of his tongue and opened the cage.

"What are you doing?" I asked.

"What does it look like?" He was hard to understand, as his tongue was still protruding from his mouth. "I'm feeding the birds."

The teal bird trotted forward and pecked the seed from his tongue.

I cringed. "That's how you feed them?"

"Not always," he replied. "Just as a special treat."

A special treat for which one of them?

"This method would be far too time-consuming to do regularly." He placed another seed on his tongue and the bird pecked it away again. He closed the cage door and faced me. "Yes."

"Yes, what?" I asked.

"I'm excited about the competition," he said. "I love live music." He did a little dance on his way to the next cage, as though to prove his enthusiasm.

"Who do you favor to win?" I asked. "Lots of people think it'll be Fat Gandalf, but I'm not so sure."

"Especially now that their drummer has died," Seymour said, his mouth forming a thin line of sympathy.

"You heard about that?" Not that I was surprised. Gossip has a way of getting around Eternal Springs, even without Skye writing about it in The Town Croaker.

Seymour fed another bird. Thankfully, this time, he used

the palm of his hand. "I try to keep my ear to the ground when it's relevant to my interests."

My radar pinged. "Oh? You mean your interest in music?" Or gambling?

Seymour looked at me askance. "Why do I have the sense you're asking more than you're actually asking?"

Well, he wasn't stupid. Just weird.

"Sorry, it's just that my interests are divided," I lied. "I want it to be a successful event because, let's face it, I organized the whole thing. At the same time, I'd like to win some money." I offered a feeble smile. "I could really use a new scooter. Mine has been on the fritz. That's why I'm walking everywhere today."

"What does money have to do with it?" Seymour asked. "Do you receive a bonus for successful events? That doesn't sound like Buddy. He's far too cheap."

I rolled my eyes. "No, it's not Buddy at all, which is why I resort to..." I gave him a cautious look. "Never mind."

"What?" he urged.

I played coy. "Let's just say I hope all the people who bet on Fat Gandalf to win don't change their minds."

Seymour appeared mildly surprised by my admission. "Ah, I see. Then I'm not alone in my pursuits."

"Manny?" I asked in a hushed voice.

"Who else?"

"Are you concerned," I asked, "now that Pete is dead?"

"I hate to sound crass, but it's good for me," Seymour said. "As long as word doesn't get out, and I get the sense you and Buddy will want to sweep the death under the carpet."

I felt a rush of indignation. "I don't want to sweep something so important under the carpet."

Seymour danced to the next cage. "Then why hasn't The Town Croaker run a story on the death?"

"Because Skye is lazy," I blurted. Ooh, I'd pay dearly for that lie if word ever got back to her.

"Yeah, I believe that," he said. He stroked the top of the bird's head.

"Were you at Anchors Away the morning it happened?" I asked in a conspiratorial whisper. Not like anyone was within earshot. We were the only two in the shop.

"I would like to have been there because, as I said, I love live music," he said. "But I was here, running the shop."

"Alone?"

He gave me a funny look. "Of course alone. I'm the only one who ever works here."

"I thought maybe you had a part-timer."

"No, and, even if I did, I wouldn't have gone. I steer clear of bars."

"Why?"

"Because I'm an alcoholic."

I recoiled. "You are?"

"Don't look so horrified," he said. "It isn't contagious."

I was mortified. I didn't mean to react so strongly to his admission. He took me off guard, that's all.

"Of course not," I said. "I just wasn't expecting you to say that. So you don't go to bars at all? Not even to meet with friends?" That seemed highly unlikely. There was no way the weird guy had friends. Guilt sat like a stone in my stomach. Now I felt guilty for thinking of him as the weird guy. He was fighting a battle no one knew about. Ugh.

"I avoid bars like I avoid cats," he said.

I raised an eyebrow. "You avoid cats?"

"You would, too, if you had all these birds." He opened his bony arms wide.

Fair point. "Did you have any customers the morning of Pete's death?"

Seymour inclined his head in that awkward manner of his.

"Are you…questioning me in your capacity as director of tourism?"

I laughed weakly. "No, of course not. I was just thinking about how lonely it must be to work alone all the time, and then I thought about our topic of conversation. The two things merged together." I tapped the side of my head. "Silly brain."

"As a matter of fact, Mrs. McNulty came in that morning. I remember distinctly because she asked me what all the fuss was about at Anchors Away. She'd ridden by there in her golf cart and noticed the commotion."

"Was she good enough to buy a bird?" I asked.

He gave me a haughty look. "She was."

I folded my arms, preparing a sharp retort.

"Skye is lazy," a bird squawked.

I whipped toward the bird. "What?"

"Skye is lazy," another bird said.

"No," I objected. "You didn't hear that."

Then every bird announced in a chorus—"Skye is lazy."

Crap!

It was easy enough to stop and verify Seymour's alibi. I knew Mrs. McNulty because she drove around in a golf cart with a picture of a mermaid painted on the side. A beautifully-rendered, accurate picture—as in no shells over the boobs. Needless to say, she was a popular sight around town with a certain crowd. There was a situation about a year ago when some of the women in town tried to force Mrs. McNulty to preserve the mermaid's modesty, but Judge Farrell dismissed the case. Victor Lamb, a lawyer in town, defended her pro bono. Apparently, he was a huge fan of the…golf cart.

I identified the infamous golf cart outside a modest bungalow. There was a wooden sign placed over top of the front door that read *What Happens at Grandma's, Stays at Grandma's*.

I strode up the path and used the knocker on the front door. I heard the shuffle of feet and an elderly woman answered the door, her silver hair still in curlers.

"Well, aren't you a pretty one?" she pronounced. "Is it Girl Scout cookie season already?"

I bit my lip. "Um, no. I'm Kenna Byrne." And I'm thirty years old. "I'm looking for Mrs. McNulty."

"Gladys is right in here," she said. "I'm Anne Kelley."

"Nice to meet you, Mrs. Kelley."

"How about a nice Irish coffee?" the old woman asked.

"Irish?"

Mrs. Kelley winked. "The liquor keeps us young. That, and routine visits to the spa for a sprinkle from the Fountain of Youth."

At least it was the water from the spa and not the carving knife of Dr. Abigail Marley.

"I'm fine, thanks. I'd just like a quick word with Mrs. McNulty and I'll be on my way."

"This way, my dear." Mrs. Kelley beckoned me forward.

I followed her through to an adjacent room where six women sat around a circular table. In the middle of the table were boxes of colored pencils, and each woman had a different coloring book.

"I'm sorry to interrupt," I said. "I didn't realize there was...an activity taking place."

"We color here every week," a white-haired woman said. "We find it soothing. This week's theme is Under the Sea, so all our books have to fit the theme."

I observed the woman's coloring of a school of fish. It looked like she'd used every colored pencil in her arsenal. I tapped the page. "You went out of the lines here."

The white-haired woman smiled at me. "It's nice to break the rules once in a while. You'll figure that out when you're older. I'm Chantelle Whitbury. This here is Margaret Middleman."

The woman beside her wiggled her fingers. "I'm Gladys McNulty and across from me is Justine Fogelman."

"And I'm Pepper Latham," a woman with long, silver hair said. It was the kind of hair that must have been glorious in her youth. Even now, I felt a surge of hair envy, despite the silver.

"We call ourselves the Widowmakers," Mrs. Whitbury said.

I blinked. "The Widowmakers? Doesn't that mean...?"

"That we killed our husbands?" Mrs. Middleman asked, and the women broke into raucous laughter. "Arguably, we sent them to early graves, but not by illegal means, honey."

Phew.

"You look vaguely familiar," Mrs. McNulty said, peering at me over her glasses.

"I'm the director of tourism for Eternal Springs," I said.

She flicked a dismissive finger. "No, that's not it." She licked her chapped lips. "Weren't you one of those nuns-in-training?"

"They're called novices," Mrs. Kelley corrected her.

"I went to St. Joan of Arc before...the unfortunate incident," I said.

What are you doing here? a strange voice asked. A yellow and white cat leaped onto the table, eyeing me suspiciously.

"Lemondrop?" I said, aghast. Lemondrop was one of the familiars from the forest that ran with Tut's gang.

"That's not Lemondrop," Mrs. Kelley said. "My cat's name is Garfield. He just loves my lasagna."

"He's the only one," Mrs. Middleman murmured.

Lemondrop/Garfield swished his tail from side to side. *I never thought I'd see any of you witches again. How's my crew?*

Your crew is fine, I said. *A little issue with excess poop in the forest, but nothing we can't handle.*

"Garfield used to show up on my back step, begging for food," Mrs. Kelley explained.

I never begged, Lemondrop said indignantly. *I only liked to hang around the back door because she'd throw away a lot of food in the compost bin.*

"Finally, I just opened the door and invited him in," Mrs. Kelley continued. "He's lived with me ever since."

"I always wanted a cat," Mrs. McNulty said. "Raymond was allergic."

"Raymond hasn't lived with you in ten years," Mrs. Latham said. "What's stopping you? Heaven knows we have a surplus of cats on this island."

"I don't know." Mrs. McNulty hesitated. "I bought a bird recently. I don't know what possessed me to do it."

Aha! "From Feathered Friends?" I asked.

Mrs. McNulty glanced at me curiously. "That's right. The weird fella sold it to me. It took all my strength not to attack his hair with the scissors in my purse."

"You're still carrying those scissors?" Mrs. Latham queried. "I told you to stop doing that. An attacker could use them against you."

Mrs. McNulty puffed out her chest. "I'd like to see him try."

"What kind of bird did you buy?" I asked, trying to steer the subject back to Feathered Friends.

"A cockatiel named Spike," she replied.

"Do you remember which morning you were there?"

"Of course I do. It was after my hair appointment with Tucker. I went straight to the bird place from there."

"Oh, I just adore Tucker," Mrs. Middleman said, fanning herself. "He can butter my biscuit anytime."

"Butter's too fattening" Mrs. Latham said. "I always use a butter substitute."

"I think you're missing the point," Mrs. Middleman replied.

"And which day was your hair appointment, Mrs. McNulty?" I asked. Trying to keep these women focused was like herding the stray cats in the forest.

"Same day as the ruckus over at Anchors Away," she said. The other women murmured in response. "Did you hear about that poor musician dying?"

"I did," I said. "It's a terrible tragedy."

"So young," Mrs. Middleman said, clucking her tongue. "His whole life still ahead of him."

"Have another fried pickle," Mrs. Kelley urged, pushing the dish toward her friend. "There's no point in holding back now."

"And where's the bird you bought?" I asked. I didn't see any evidence of one.

"In my bedroom," she replied. "I like company in the evenings when I go to bed. We read a book together before I fall asleep."

"The bird reads?" I asked.

"He sits on my shoulder and it seems like he's reading," Mrs. McNulty said. "Do you have any pets?"

I dreaded this question almost as much as I dreaded questions about my love life. "I do."

"A dog?" Mrs. Latham asked. "You strike me as a poodle person. They're very fussy."

I balked. "I'm not fussy."

"You've color coordinated your ensemble within an inch of your life," Mrs. Latham said. "That's what I call fussy."

"I don't have a poodle, or any dog for that matter," I said.

"I suppose it's a cat then," Mrs. Kelley said. "They make such excellent companions."

"Actually, I have an armadillo," I said.

The women gaped at me.

"Why on earth would you have one of those?" Mrs. Latham asked.

"It's a long story," I said.

"Is it a religious thing?" Mrs. Middleman asked.

"No, I'm not aware of any religion that involves armadillos," I said.

"Oh, I'll bet there is," Mrs. McNulty said. "You're just not looking hard enough."

I frowned. "Well, I'm not really looking at all."

"For a boyfriend?" Mrs. Kelley asked, chomping on a fried pickle. "Are you fixed for one of those? I'm partial to Dirk Jenkins down at the rec center, but these ladies don't think he's up to snuff."

"He smells like glue," Mrs. Latham objected. "A grown man shouldn't smell like glue."

"He's a handyman," Mrs. Kelley said. "It seems perfectly natural to me."

"You just make excuses so you can justify the relationship," Mrs. McNulty said.

"I don't need to justify anything," Mrs. Kelley said plainly. "Mark my words, young lady, when you get to be our age, reasoning goes out the window. We do as we please and to hell with anyone's opinion."

"You'd like my friend Skye," I said.

"If you don't mind me asking, how did you know to find me here?" Mrs. McNulty asked.

"I recognized your golf cart," I said.

"Of course. Who doesn't?" Mrs. McNulty sighed. "Some days I want to take a spray can to the whole thing."

"What's stopping you?" I asked.

She tugged on a fine chin hair. "For one thing, my late husband painted that picture. I'd feel terrible defacing it."

"Oh, I'm so sorry," I said. "I didn't realize."

She waved me off. "It isn't so much affection for him as it is for the picture. He painted it of me."

"You?" I echoed.

"Hard to believe, isn't it?" She smiled. "My boobs have been strongly influenced by gravity since then, but once upon a time..." She pursed her chapped lips. "I like seeing myself in my prime. Sometimes it's like looking in the mirror. For a split second, I forget my age. I forget how much time has passed."

"It's a nice reminder," I said. "We should all be so lucky to have a painting like that."

"You should have one done now," she said, glancing at my chest, "while your boobs are still perky."

"I appreciate the thought," I said. "I'm not sure that I'm as adventurous as you were. Besides, I don't have an artistic husband." Or any type of husband, for that matter.

"I don't see why you can't commission it," Mrs. McNulty said. "Any virile young painter would be more than happy to paint you topless. Trust me. They act like it's all about art, but before you know it, your skirt's wrapped around your waist and your legs are in the air." She blushed profusely. "Forgive me. It's been quite some time."

Mrs. Kelley winked. "A handyman's looking pretty good about now, isn't he?"

Chapter Nine

I sat at the desk in my office, trying to force myself to concentrate. Although the Battle of the Bands was imminent, the murder was taking over my schedule in a way that I didn't like, not to mention I hadn't done anything about the flying monkeys. What if someone spotted them before I had a chance to eradicate them? My compulsion was for things to run smoothly, but these extracurricular activities were interfering with that goal.

An insistent knock snapped me back to earth.

"What is it, Dottie?" Dottie Hayes was my sixty-five-year-old assistant. She'd also served as the assistant to my predecessor, Cyril Rhodes. I'd worked as a manager under Cyril until his retirement, when Buddy promoted me to director. When I gave Dottie the option to stay, she did. The woman was borderline crazy, but she was as dedicated to her job as I was to mine. I knew that was a rare find, so I wasn't inclined to replace her.

The door opened and Dottie entered the office, her cherry red hair styled in a bouffant worthy of The B-52s. "There's a cat here to see you, doll. Should I show him in?"

My brow lifted. "A cat?" Only someone as crazy as Dottie would say this as though it were perfectly normal. Then again, she was accustomed to my pink fairy armadillo and the albino raven that followed me everywhere. She mistakenly believed I was as eccentric as she was, rather than a witch.

"Well, at least I think it's a cat." She scratched her foundation-encrusted cheek. "It's got no hair and it looks at me like it understands me, which is mighty impressive because most people don't seem capable of that."

A hairless cat? That could only mean Tut, the self-appointed alpha of the cat pack. What was Tut doing here? He wouldn't normally bother me at the office. He was more of a home invader, stepping out of the shadows and scaring the pants off me.

"I have a few minutes to spare," I said. "Show him in."

Dottie wrinkled her nose. "I don't suppose he wants coffee or tea. Should I offer him a saucer of milk?"

Bless her heart. "You can offer, but I don't think he's partial to milk." I knew for a fact that Tut liked to lick the empty beer bottles outside places like Coconuts and Anchors Away. I caught him lurking amongst the garbage bins one time too many.

Dottie disappeared for a brief moment and returned with Tut hot on her heels. He jumped up into the chair across from my desk and made himself comfortable.

"Thanks, Dottie," I said. "Would you mind closing the door behind you?" I didn't need anyone overhearing my conversation with the hairless cat. For one thing, they would only hear my end of it because regular humans can't hear the animals speak. Like the sarcastic trees, it was more of a witch thing.

"This must be serious for you to come all the way to my office," I said.

"I'm here to lodge a formal complaint," Tut said with an air of authority.

I braided my fingers together. "Is that so? And what's the issue?"

Tut fixed me with his slanted cat eyes. "There's been an excess of excrement in the forest as of late. It has become a nuisance. The cats can't take a step without fear of an unexpected visit to Pooptown."

I frowned. "Why the formal complaint?"

"You're in charge of tourism here," Tut explained. "It's your job to keep everything nice. Tourists don't want to be wandering through the woods and dodging poop patties wherever they walk. The smell wasn't so great, either, I'll have you know."

He had a point. Tourists did like to partake in hikes and other nature-based activities.

"The cats are concerned that there are animals encroaching on our territory," Tut continued. "One of the kittens came home the other day, completely coated in it. His mother was none too pleased."

I opened my mouth to respond, but Tut continued.

"Before you offer up a reasonable reply, it's not big enough to belong to a Great Dane, if that's what you're thinking," Tut said.

"What does a Great Dane have to do with me?" It wasn't like Lucas and I were dating or anything. We'd only run into each other a couple of times.

"We've seen you spending time with the Shirtless Wonder and his mighty steed," Tut replied.

"I don't know anyone with a horse," I said, being deliberately obtuse.

"You know exactly who I mean," Tut said, retracting his claws and popping them out again for affect.

"Put those away," I admonished him. "You know you can't

intimidate me. That chair will become electric faster than you can say cat." I wiggled my index finger in a menacing manner.

Tut relaxed back into the chair. "The dog and her shirtless friend have been coming to the forest for years. We're familiar with her feces."

Inwardly, I groaned. I couldn't believe this was the conversation I was having. I seriously hoped Dottie wasn't eavesdropping.

"Listen, I have information for you, but you need to remain calm," I said.

Tut's ears perked up. "*You* have information for *me*?"

"It happens on occasion." I cleared my throat. "The truth is I'm glad you came by because I've needed to talk to you. Apparently, there are flying monkeys at large."

Tut froze. "Flying monkeys?"

"That's right," I said. "I'm surprised you haven't noticed them in the forest. That's where they seem to be congregating at the moment."

"It's a rather big wooded area," Tut said defensively. "I take it they're from..."

I nodded. "I'll get rid of them, I promise. Just keep the little ones on a tight leash for now. Maybe institute a curfew until the matter's been resolved."

"And when will that be?" Tut inquired. "You know wrangling cats isn't easy."

"I can't give you a date," I said. "My time is a little on the tight side at the moment."

"Because of the murder?"

I blew out an annoyed breath. "How do you know about that?"

"Because I was peering over Skye's shoulder at her house while she wrote about it."

My whole body tensed. "You saw Skye writing an article

about Pete's murder?" That filthy witch! She knew perfectly well she needed to wait to run that story. It would reflect negatively on the competition, as well as the town. I couldn't have that.

Tut dug his claws into the upholstery of the chair. "Who's Kyle Charney?"

"Kyle Charney?" I echoed. "He's the tax assessor for the northern quadrant. Why?" What on earth did Kyle Charney have to do with anything?

Tut retracted his claws again, leaving tiny holes in the fabric. "I have no idea, but his name is mentioned in the article. I suppose you should ask Skye."

Right now, I would rather wash my eyes with bleach, but I needed any information Skye had. I had no choice but to pay her a visit.

"Thanks for stopping by," I said. "Next time it might be better if you visit me at home." Not that I wanted that either, but I also didn't want rumors circulating at the office about strange visits from a hairless cat.

"As you wish," Tut said, and promptly jumped down from the chair. I watched in fascination as he stood on his hind legs, jiggled the doorknob with both paws, and let himself out. He was so competent—if he weren't a feral cat, I'd probably hire him.

IT DIDN'T TAKE ME LONG TO TRACK DOWN THE WIND witch. In typical Skye fashion, she was still at home in her pajamas. As far as I was concerned, the witch had no work ethic and even fewer organizational skills. The second the front door opened, a winged creature zoomed toward me, skimming over the top of my head.

"Swoops!" I shouted. "That bat is a menace to hairstyles everywhere."

Skye appeared in the doorway, laughing. "It's an improvement from where I'm standing."

I smoothed my dark hair. "I want to see the article your writing," I demanded.

Skye's expression shifted to one of complete innocence. "What article? The one on the opening of Mary Lou's chiropractic clinic? I'd be happy to share it with you, but it isn't finished yet."

I folded my arms. "You know exactly which article I'm referring to. I explicitly asked you not to cover the murder right now. The competition is days away. You'll completely ruin the event if you publish a story about a murder connected to it."

"The news is the news," Skye said. "People deserve to know if there's a murderer afoot."

Swoops raced back through the open door, nearly knocking the earring straight out of my earlobe. *Hungry*, the bat said. *On verge of total collapse*.

"Don't you ever feed this poor bat?" I asked.

Skye shot him a warning look. "What do you think? You don't get as chubby as him without more food than you need."

"Now that you mention it, Swoops does look a bit heavier than the last time I saw him."

Skye stared at me. "That's offensive and rude."

"What? You mentioned it first."

Skye eyed me the way I looked at Dottie when she came to the office wearing go-go boots and a mini-dress.

"By the way," I said quickly. "You're on Zola's list because of the candle wax prank."

"I'm pretty sure that was you, fire witch."

"Nice try. Zola and I figured it out, so you may want to make it up to her before she finds a way to repay you."

"Since when do you two put your heads together?" she asked, a note of suspicion creeping into her voice.

"I went looking for cackleberries, which apparently you cleaned out of the forest. Zola didn't have a batch ready either." I didn't mention the incident with Clover. The last thing I needed was Skye knowing about the problem in the forest. Knowing her, she'd probably conjure up a strong gust of wind to bring the stench downtown the day of the competition.

"What can I say? A girl has needs."

I have needs, Swoops said, sailing past us. *Dietary needs.*

"Tell me about Kyle Charney," I said.

"The tax assessor? I'm pretty sure he's married. Why, are you interested?" Skye batted her eyes. No, she couldn't make this easy, could she?

I rolled my eyes. I didn't have time to mess around. My To-Do list was far too lengthy at this point. "Name your price," I said.

"How about another rendition of *Total Eclipse of the Heart* on karaoke night?"

Coconuts hosted karaoke every Friday night. Although I don't usually sing in public, Skye had accidentally spelled the rum runners, which resulted in an evening of '80s power ballads. I was still living down that night. I even heard the janitor humming the familiar bars of the Bonnie Tyler song when he was mopping the floor behind me the other night.

"No way," I said. "Something else." *Anything* else...except country. I draw the line at country music.

Skye smiled. "Okay, fine. How about a song of your choosing?"

I huffed. "No karaoke, Skye."

She doubled down. "No karaoke, no Kyle Charney. See how that works?"

I resisted the urge to shake my fist at her. She knew she had me. "Paybacks are a witch," I said. I felt a brief moment of satisfaction when I saw the fear flicker in her eyes. Just as quickly, it was gone.

"It turns out that Kyle Charney has been hired to replace Pete Simpson as the drummer for Fat Gandalf."

The dumpy tax assessor was a part-time rock-n-roll drummer?

"So you think that's a motive for murder? The local tax assessor desperately wanted to be the drummer in a local band that may or may not win a competition?"

Skye shrugged. "If I've learned one thing in my years of reporting, it's that people do things for dumbass reasons. What you or I would consider a strong motive isn't necessarily relevant."

Fair point. "Have you spoken to him?"

"Not yet," she said. "I only got the tip yesterday. When I went by his house, he wasn't there."

"Perfect, thanks," I said. With Skye still in pajamas, I had plenty of time to track down Kyle before she did. "I'm going to ask you one more time. Please hold off on publishing a story about Pete's death until after the competition."

"Buddy is already annoyed about the negative gossip," Skye said. "You want me to forgo the opportunity to turn the screw?" She clucked her tongue.

"He'll have a heart attack if you publish a story that ruins the competition that the town has invested so much money in," I said.

"Let's be honest. Would Buddy having a heart attack really be such a bad thing?" she queried. "I don't even think his wife would be upset, unless she was put in charge of the bed pan."

I disliked Buddy as much as anybody else, but he was also

my boss in a convoluted way and I generally endeavored not to piss him off.

"We had a deal, Skye," I said. "How about I ask Zola not to return the favor of pranking you?"

Skye made a show of examining her stubby fingernails. "I'll hold off on the story on one condition."

Uh oh. This didn't bode well for me. I could feel it in my bones. "What is it?"

"You invite Skywalker to Coconuts for karaoke night," she said smugly.

My eyes popped. "How do you know about Lucas?"

She smirked. "I'm the town reporter, remember? It's my job to know things."

"I barely know him," I said. "What's the point of inviting him?"

"Ah, but you *want* to know him," she said. "So that ramps up the embarrassment factor to a higher, more enjoyable level."

"He's a really nice guy, Skye," I said. "And we were awful to him."

"So you want to pity date him, is that it?"

"I don't pity him," I said quickly.

Her eyes lit up. "But you do want to date him. I knew it! My sources are always good." She flicked an invisible piece of lint off my shoulder. "Invite Skywalker to your big performance or the deal's off."

I couldn't possibly invite Lucas to Coconuts, especially when I was being forced to sing karaoke. He'd never want to see me again. It suddenly occurred to me that I didn't want that to happen. On the other hand, I desperately needed Skye to hold off on the story for the good of the town, not to mention for the good of my job. A failed Battle of the Bands competition could mean the loss of my job. Buddy would have blinders on when it came to all the good I'd done before this. He would only be able to focus on what was right in front of him. Like a toddler.

"Fine, I'll do it," I said. I regretted the words the moment they passed my lips, but there was nothing I could do about it. I fled Skye's house and went in search of Kyle Charney.

Chapter Ten

Just my luck that Kyle Charney was assessing houses in the northern quadrant. I called that area of the island the tundra because the temperature there was *much* colder than the part of town where I lived, and I hated the cold with a fiery passion...which made sense given that I was a fire witch.

I stopped by my house to grab a coat and hat. The wind alone would be frigid without extra layers. I ran upstairs to find Gerald in my bedroom, curled up on the bottom edge of the bed. He looked so adorable that I slowed my pace so as not to disturb him.

When I opened the closet door, I let out a shriek of dismay. My clothes were in disarray—a black top hung beside a green one, while two red tops were interrupted by a blue top. It was anarchy! Worst of all, my freshly laundered jeans were in a crumpled in a heap on the floor.

"Gerald," I yelled at the top of my lungs, forgetting he was asleep on the bed behind me.

The armadillo cracked his sleepy eyes and peered at me. *Is it a mouse?*

"No, it is not a mouse, but thank you for putting that image in my head." Gerald knows that mice are a secret fear of mine. Their little flexible endoskeletons freaked me out.

He fluttered over to the closet. *What happened in here?*

"That's what I'm asking you. I thought you were going to perfect the organizational spell. This is the opposite of perfect."

I was busy researching the flying monkey issue today. I didn't bother with the organizational spell. It must've been that Stuart, trying to frame me.

"You can't blame it on Stuart," I said. "He's not even smart enough to find a way into the house undetected."

It wasn't me, I swear it, miss, Gerald said. He paused. *Actually, I take it back. I did begin a color coordination spell but got distracted by a package delivery. Your monthly vegetable box.*

"Great, thanks," I said distractedly. "I need to find my coat, but everything's out of order." The cottons were even mixed with the synthetics. It was a textiles nightmare.

I thought you kept your coat with the Rarely Used Items, Gerald pointed out.

I snapped my fingers. "You're right. Well done, Gerald. All is forgiven." I hurried downstairs to the closet under the stairs, where I stored any items I *might* need one day, like a pair of Rollerblades or a chef's apron. Or a coat.

Why do you need a coat? Gerald asked, as I slipped on the warm and cozy eggplant-colored coat. *You despise the cold.*

"I have to beat Skye to the tundra to question a suspect," I said.

A suspect? Shouldn't you leave that to Buddy?

I cocked an eyebrow. "Leave work to Buddy? You can't be serious. That man can't find a fourteen-inch knitting needle in his wife's yarn basket. He's still waiting for the toxicology results before he's willing to label the death suspicious."

Fair enough, miss.

"The Battle of the Bands has to go off without a hitch," I said, feeling my anxiety level rise. "If the only thing people can talk about is Pete's unsolved murder, that will ruin the event. I wanted this to be the first of an annual event, not a one-time only."

Be sure to wear your gloves, miss, Gerald advised. *You know how your fingers get stiff in the cold. Makes it hard to do magic if you need to.*

I patted his silky head. "That's why you're my familiar, Gerald. You're always looking out for me." I pulled a pair of gloves from my coat pocket and slipped them on. "If you see Stuart lurking around the house, tell him that his guerrilla warfare tactics won't work."

I acknowledged that the closet wasn't due to Stuart, miss.

"Oh, right. That you did. Sorry. My mind is in fifty places right now."

Permission to Taser him anyway? Gerald asked hopefully.

I squinted at my pink fairy armadillo. "Since when do you have a Taser?"

Not an actual Taser, Gerald said. *A little fairy stun magic. Works like a charm.*

"You're in charge," I said. "Use whatever force you deem necessary."

Gerald's wings fluttered rapidly, his excitement evident. *I'll have hot cocoa ready for your return.*

"You're the best," I called over my shoulder.

THE RIDE TO THE NORTHERN END OF THE ISLAND TOOK longer than I anticipated. I should've worn a ski mask instead of a hat. I was fairly certain there were icicles under my nose. It's no mystery that this part of the island has the fewest inhabitants. What is a mystery is why anyone chooses to live here at all.

HOTTER THAN SPELL

It wasn't difficult to locate Kyle Charney. His bright orange golf cart had the Eternal Springs logo painted on the side. I noticed that it didn't identify him as the tax assessor, though, which I was sure was a strategic move. He didn't want people to see him coming and refuse to answer their doors. Property taxes weren't ridiculously expensive like they are on the mainland, especially New Jersey—how anyone could live there, I'd never understand. Even so, nobody wanted Kyle to come knocking and end the day with an increase in their annual property taxes.

I waited by his golf cart, uncertain which of the houses on the street he was assessing now. They appeared to be identical houses in an assortment of colors. There must have been a homeowners' association rule that no neighboring houses could share the same exterior paint color.

My breath came out as mist thanks to the cold. I danced around on the sidewalk to keep myself warm, resisting the urge to use magic. I didn't want to do anything that would draw attention to myself. Goddess knew we did enough of that thirteen years ago. I tried to keep my magic to a minimum. I didn't trust the reaction of island residents should my secret ever get out.

Kyle emerged from the house to my left, swaddled in a down jacket and clutching a clipboard. He glanced up in surprise at the sight of me.

"Kenna?" he asked. "What are you doing all the way out here?"

"I'm the director of tourism for the entire island, Kyle, not just the good part...I mean, the warm part." I cleared my throat. "Once in a blue moon, I take a tour to see how I can maximize our best features."

"That's an excellent idea," Kyle said. "I'd be happy to offer suggestions. I spend a lot of time out here. My wife thinks we should move to this end of the island, to make my commute easier."

He drove a golf cart to work on roads that were generally free of traffic. How much easier could his commute get?

"You'd still need to come to the administrative office," I said.

"That's what I told her. Besides, I like the ride. I do my best thinking driving out here and back again. Blue skies, the sounds of the ocean. It doesn't get much better than this."

Kyle didn't sound like someone eager to quit and tour the country with a band.

"I can't imagine living anywhere else," I lied. "Eternal Springs has everything a person could ever want."

He continued to his golf cart and set his clipboard on the passenger seat before pulling a flask of hot coffee from the back. "You really love your job, don't you?"

"Of course. Don't you?" I asked.

His hesitation spoke volumes. So maybe I was mistaken. "Mine's not the most popular job in town."

Of course. It was the job itself, not the commute or the location. "Because you're the tax assessor?"

"Yeah. I'm about as popular as burnt toast," he said glumly. He took a cautious sip from his flask and offered it to me, but I waved him off.

"No, thank you. I don't...like coffee." In truth, I didn't share drinks, or food, for that matter. The idea of someone else's germs finding their way into my mouth...I winced. It was bad enough the other witches knew about my strong feelings on the subject. During the years, they'd hatched plenty of schemes involving switched coffee mugs and licked straws in the hope of watching me melt down. Most of the time, I managed to hold it together. Anything to deny them the satisfaction.

"You're in charge of the Battle of the Bands competition, aren't you?" His face brightened at the mention of it.

"That's right," I said. "Will you be attending?"

His head bobbed up and down enthusiastically. "Not just attending. I'm competing."

"Is that right? I didn't know you were in a band." A necessary lie.

"I was the drummer for Unpaid Interns," he said. "But they decided not to play the competition."

"Why not?"

He blew a raspberry. "Too much competition, apparently. They knew they didn't have a shot with all these great bands flying in."

"Then how are you in it?"

"I've replaced the drummer for Fat Gandalf," he said. "They needed someone quickly and I was ready and able."

I pretended to be shocked. "The one who died? Pete?"

"That's the one," Kyle said. "Poor guy. So close to his big break." He shook his head sadly. "You were there when it happened, weren't you? I thought I remembered seeing you."

"You were there?"

"I stopped by on my way to work to check out some of the bands," he said. "I talked to Keith and mentioned how my band was sitting out."

"And he remembered?"

"Yeah, can you believe it?" Kyle asked. "He came looking for me to ask if I wanted to be their new drummer. It was like Christmas and my birthday rolled into one." He rubbed his hands together in an effort to stay warm.

"Is that your dream?" I asked. "To be the drummer in a band?"

"I love music," he said, "but I also want to be popular for a change, you know? In high school, I was a band geek, which on the popularity scale is pretty low. Then I became a tax assessor, the person everyone hides from. On stage with a band...it's different." He got a faraway look in his eyes. "People clapping and cheering. They're *happy* to see me."

"You want to quit your job and tour with the band," I said, more of a statement than a question.

"Absolutely," he said. "As much as I love Eternal Springs, that's the real dream." He sighed. "And I'm this close to making it come true." He held his index finger and thumb an inch apart.

I thought about Tiffany and her resistance to Pete's dream. "What about your wife? Does she support you?"

"One hundred percent," Kyle said. "We're practicing like crazy this week and she's been a real trooper. I'm a lucky man."

"I'll bet," I said. Kyle certainly had motive and opportunity, but my gut told me that he didn't have the stomach for murder. "Where were you when Fat Gandalf was playing onstage during the practice session?"

Kyle's eyes glistened with excitement. "At the foot of the stage with Steve's girlfriend and his mother, Lila. Lila and I are in the same bridge group."

My brow lifted. "You play bridge?" With old women? And Kyle wondered why he wasn't more popular.

"My grandmother taught me bridge and my father taught me how to play the drums," he said.

"Is your grandmother in the group, too?" I asked.

His head drooped. "No, she passed a few years ago. That's why I joined Lila's group. I missed playing with Nana Jo."

Sweet Goddess of mine. There was no way this guy killed Pete. He was simply reveling in his good fortune.

"So if Fat Gandalf wins, is the plan to use the money to tour?" I asked.

Kyle nodded. "We'll make an album first, then a North

American tour. I can't say I'll be sad to give my notice." He entwined his index and middle fingers. "Fingers crossed."

I copied the gesture. "Fingers crossed for you, Kyle." I found that I meant it. "Officially, I have to remain impartial, of course, but I'll be cheering you on."

He beamed. "Thanks, Kenna. I don't know why everyone says you're such a…" He trailed off, thinking better of his intended statement. "Serious woman. It's obvious you have a fun side." It was a feeble recovery, but I let it go.

"I need to get a move on before I freeze to death," I said. "It was nice chatting with you, Kyle."

As I walked back to my scooter, my body was so stiff with cold that I could barely lift my bottom onto the seat. I waited until Kyle had moved on before focusing my magic on myself. I pictured a steaming sauna and chanted quietly, "Never fear, never doubt. Warm this body from the inside out."

My muscles immediately relaxed as my body temperature rose. By the time I crossed the border into downtown, my winter clothes were neatly placed in the scooter's basket.

I groaned when I recognized the golf cart in front of me. Buddy.

I pulled alongside him and beeped my horn in greeting. Mitzi sat in the passenger seat beside him, intent on her knitting. The sight nearly sent me into a deep slumber, so accustomed was I to using her knitting show as a sleep aid.

"Kenna Byrne, just the lady I wanted to see," Buddy said, bringing his golf cart to a stop.

Magic and mayhem, those were not words I wanted to hear.

I stopped my scooter beside his cart. "How can I help you, Buddy?" I asked, injecting just the right amount of sweetness into my tone.

"You've got to clamp down on this gossip about Pete,"

Buddy said. "It's going to make a mess of the competition. All that money we've put into the event will be wasted."

I wasn't sure how I could put a stop to island gossip. "I'm doing what I can." Unlike you, I thought.

"I've been thinking about doing a little number at the start of the competition," Buddy said. "I used to play the saxophone, you know."

"And the harmonica," Mitzi added, without looking up from her knitting.

I pressed my lips together. "The sax *and* the harmonica? A double threat." Now if he could play them both at the same time, *that* would be impressive. And it would prevent him from talking.

"I've been debating it because, well, I don't want to show up the competitors," Buddy said. When it came to music or politics, or basically anything at all, the mayor was his own biggest fan.

"That's a good point," I said. "You don't want to detract from the musicians. They might feel so outshone by you that they decide not to bother competing."

Mitzi tapped her husband's arm with a knitting needle. "I told you. You're the sun, Buddy. You'll burn too brightly for that group."

Or he was just full of gas.

Buddy smiled at his wife. "My biggest fan."

I couldn't tell whether Mitzi was serious or simply placating her egotistical husband.

"Your wife is right," I said. "It wouldn't be fair."

Buddy rubbed his chin. "I am kind of a big deal. I just hate to deprive residents of the chance to hear me play."

"Maybe next year," I said. "We'll work it into the schedule."

"If there *is* a next year," Buddy grumbled. "If this Pete

Simpson nonsense doesn't die down, there won't be a competition next year."

"Die down?" I repeated.

"That's a poor choice of words," Mitzi said.

Buddy snatched his wife's knitting needle and pointed it at me. "Get a handle on the situation, Kenna. I'd hate to have to start thinking about your replacement."

I gritted my teeth, fighting the temptation to set Buddy's golf cart ablaze. Maybe I'd settle for his toupee.

"I'll do my best," I said tersely, and started the scooter's engine.

"That's what I like about you, Kenna," he called after me. "You always do."

Chapter Eleven

After my annoying run-in with Buddy, I decided to bypass the office and go home. Who was he to tell me to put a cork in island chatter? I had as much at stake as he did, but why was it *my* job to quash it? All four witches together didn't have the power to stop people from gossiping.

I fished my key out of my pocket and was about to unlock the front door when I heard someone call my name. My head whipped toward the sound and I saw a shirtless Lucas jogging along the sidewalk, Leia gracefully trotting beside him. I'd have mocked his shirtless habit if his abs weren't so sculpted and enticing. No reason to give the guy a complex and force him to cover up.

"Hey," he said, approaching my front porch. He hadn't even broken a sweat. Leia settled in the shade of a nearby tree.

"Hi, how are you?" I glanced around furtively for Stuart, hoping he was nowhere to be seen.

"Pretty good." He noticed the winter clothes tucked under my arm. "Wow. I bet you overheated today."

With my eyes locked on those abs, I *was* in serious danger of overheating. "I had to go north today."

"You should've told me," he said. "I could've flown you."

"No, thank you," I said quickly.

He didn't miss my rapid response. "That's right. You're a big fan of gravity. Now I remember."

"You wouldn't want to fly me anywhere," I said. "I imagine I might get sick or something."

"You imagine?" His eyes widened. "You mean you've never been on an airplane?"

Mother of magic. "No, I haven't." I'd come to the island by boat when I was younger in order to attend St. Joan of Arc.

He broke into a broad grin. "I didn't realize you were a virgin." His cheeks flamed. "I mean, that you've never flown at all. We need to remedy that as soon as possible."

"We really don't, but I appreciate the sentiment." I unlocked the door. "Can I offer you a glass of water? You look like you could use a drink."

"I wouldn't say no to a drink," he said. He turned toward the Great Dane. "Leia, stay."

The command was only for show. Leia was perfectly content under the tree.

"I can bring her a bowl of water," I said.

Leia barked as though responding to my offer.

Lucas and I entered the house and I immediately called out to Gerald to make it clear that we had company. I didn't need him fluttering into the room and casting a spell. Lucas already had to think my choice in pets was strange. No one else had a pink fairy armadillo.

"Do you feed that odd-looking bird or something?" Lucas asked. "I see it every time I pass your house."

"Stuart?" I queried.

Lucas looked perplexed. "The random bird has a name?"

"That's just what I call him," I said, recovering quickly.

"He's an albino raven. I think he's partial to the berries in my backyard."

How often is Mr. Ab-tastic passing our house that he's noticed Stuart? Gerald asked.

I ignored Gerald. I wasn't even sure where my familiar was hiding in the house.

Don't call him that, I said. *You sound like Tut.*

I went into the kitchen and filled a bowl with water for Leia and a glass for Lucas.

"Do you always jog through this neighborhood?" I asked. I certainly would've noticed if he did.

"It's a new route," Lucas said, gulping down the water. "I like to mix things up on occasion or I get bored."

"I see." Maybe that explained his apparent interest in me. I was his attempt to mix things up until he got bored. That didn't seem out of the realm of possibility for a guy who flew airplanes for a living. He wanted excitement and adventure. I wanted a schedule that never changed. It would never pan out between us.

"I'll bring this to Leia," he said, taking the bowl. "Thanks."

I waited in the kitchen, trying to keep my heartbeat steady. What did it matter if he liked to mix things up? I wasn't looking for a long-term relationship. How could I? My identity was secret and it had to stay that way. If I got too close to Lucas—to anyone—I risked exposing my witchy sisters as well as myself. As much as they annoyed me, I would never risk outing them to the rest of Eternal Springs. It would likely end badly for all of us. The residents wouldn't react kindly to four witches in their backyard. They'd probably overlook the fact that we were protecting them from hellish creatures like flying monkeys and skip right to burning us at the stake.

Gerald came around the corner, his bottom rising and falling as his wings attempted to hold his weight aloft.

The front door opened and closed, alerting me to Lucas's return. "I heard some gossip on the plane this morning that might interest you," he said.

"Gerald, your wings," I hissed, motioning downward with my hand. "We have company."

Oh, right. Apologies, miss. Gerald dropped to all fours on the floor and smoothed his wings so they blended with his body.

Lucas stopped short when he spied Gerald. "There's your armadillo. Hey, buddy." He stopped to pet Gerald's back as though he were a garden-variety cat or dog.

His hand feels strong, Gerald said with a deep sigh.

"What's the gossip?" I asked, ignoring Gerald.

"I flew a group in from the mainland today," Lucas said. "One of the bands for the competition."

There were only a handful that hadn't yet arrived. I took a shot in the dark. "Look Mom, No Wings? Drunk Pandas?"

"Nameless Faces," Lucas said.

I snapped my fingers. "Right. They're supposed to be awesome."

"Turns out they played a gig in New York with Fat Gandalf a couple of months ago."

"Oh, nice," I said.

"They were a little shaken up because they'd heard about Pete's death," Lucas said. "And the guitarist mentioned seeing Pete backstage with a woman at the show."

"With a woman?" I repeated. "Like *with* her?"

"Making out like high school kids, apparently," Lucas said.

I inclined my head. "Did you make out a lot in high school?" I couldn't imagine Skywalker getting many opportunities, not with his lightsaber getting in the way.

His cheeks flushed again. "Not really. Anyway, the making out isn't the important part."

"It might be to his wife," I said.

Lucas's gaze met mine. "According to the guitarist, he was making out with *a* wife, just not his. It was Keith's."

My eyebrows shot up. "Rachel Simonson?" I couldn't picture the sleek blonde with messy hair and smeared lipstick. She was too much like...me.

Lucas nodded. "The guitarist said those two seemed very familiar with each other, like it wasn't the first time they'd hooked up."

I wondered whether it was the last. "Thanks for the tip," I said. "I'll be sure to pass it along." To myself, because there was no way I was giving Buddy critical intel like that. He'd find a way to rationalize it and dismiss it.

"I figured you'd want to know," Lucas said.

I certainly did. "I guess you've flown a lot of the bands to the island."

"Not all of them," he said. "Some prefer to arrive by boat."

"I can understand that preference," I said.

Lucas laughed. "I'll take you one day and turn your world upside down. Literally."

My stomach grew nauseated just thinking about it.

"You'll love it," he insisted. "There's nothing quite like being above the clouds."

Although I knew there was no way I'd feel the same, I didn't want to dampen his enthusiasm.

"Did you always want to be a pilot?" I asked.

"Not particularly. Mostly I wanted to get away," he said.

"I thought that was why you went to the forest," I said.

"That was before I was old enough to get my license. I still go there, to mix things up," he replied. "But taking to the skies and leaving the island behind...It's so peaceful and quiet up there." He became lost in thought. "Sometimes I need that distance. It's how I cope."

Cope with what? I wanted to ask, but kept the question to myself. It felt too personal.

"You make it sound very tempting," I said. Then again, everything about Lucas was tempting.

Like Adam and his apple, Gerald said.

Gerald! Out of my head, I snapped. I was more interested in Adam's banana than his apple.

"Um, I'm glad you're here, actually, because there's something I need to ask you," I said. Great balls of magical fire, I hated Skye more than hemorrhoids right now.

Lucas eyed me curiously. "If you want me to demonstrate how Pete and Rachel were making out, I'm afraid the answer is no. I wasn't there, so I couldn't possibly show you."

Now it was my turn to blush. "Ha ha. Very funny. No, I was wondering if you ever go to Coconuts on karaoke night."

His brow creased. "Karaoke night? Why? Is that a tourist attraction?"

"More of a local attraction, but we do get an influx of tourists every so often, depending on what's happening in town."

"Why do you ask?" Lucas said. He raised his arm and leaned against the top of the door frame. Sweet Goddess above, that was a serious bicep near my face. I wondered what would happen if I just pressed my lips against it... "Kenna?"

I snapped to attention. "Oh, yes. Um, I'll be performing at karaoke night on Friday, so if you're interested in a good laugh, please come by."

He gave me a lopsided grin. "You're performing? What song?"

"Not sure yet," I said.

"You don't seem very happy about it," he said.

"I kind of lost a bet," I said. I couldn't tell him the truth.

Skye wouldn't want anyone to know she sat on stories and I didn't want anyone to know I asked her to. We both wanted our integrity to remain intact.

"Sounds like a fun time," he said. "I'll see if I can make it."

I admit, my heartbeat skidded to a halt when he didn't respond with a resounding yes. Was he playing hard to get? Or was he just not interested?

What does it matter if you don't really like him, miss? Gerald asked.

For the last time, get out of my head, Gerald! I glared at my familiar and he slunk off to the living room.

"If you hear any more gossip from the bands, would you let me know?" I asked.

"Sure thing." He headed toward the door and stopped as a ball of feathers shot past the front door. "I think that weird bird is back. Maybe you should contact pest control or something. It seems like a real nuisance."

He has no idea, Gerald said dryly.

"He's harmless," I assured him. "Thanks for stopping by."

Lucas paused on the porch. "Is that okay? I mean, I don't make a habit of dropping by people's houses unannounced. I'm not a creeper." He cast a sidelong glance. "Like that bird."

I gave him my most encouraging smile. "It's totally fine, Lucas."

Your lip is stuck to your front tooth, miss, Gerald advised.

I clamped my mouth closed and Lucas's brow wrinkled.

"Good luck with the competition," Lucas said. "I hope it's a huge success."

"Thanks. Me, too." And I had far too much riding on it to fail.

As soon as Lucas and Leia were gone, I spun around and faced Gerald. "We need to do a locator spell on Keith Simonson."

Actually, miss, I've been working on our flying monkey problem. I found a spell that can…

I waved him off. "Monkeys have to wait. I need to find Keith. If he found out that Rachel and Pete were having an affair, he could be the killer."

Forgive me, miss, but wasn't he on the stage when you found the victim?

"Yes, but no one knows how long Pete was on the floor," I argued. "Keith could've killed him and then rushed to the stage."

An excellent point, miss. If I could show you the information I found regarding the monkeys first… .

"There's no time, Gerald. I'm all about multi-tasking, you know that, but I need to strike while the iron's hot." And while Skye and I had a deal. The minute I sang karaoke, all bets were off.

To the bat cave then, miss?

"You know I don't call it that, Gerald. You're not Swoops."

Thank goodness for that.

I pulled Jane Austen's *Sense and Sensibility* off the shelf and a secret door opened. Most people would have chosen *Pride and Prejudice*, but I had a soft spot for the Dashwood sisters, Elinor and Marianne.

Gerald and I entered the small room that I used for practicing magic. I couldn't take the risk of someone noticing my extracurricular activities—someone like Lucas.

A spell book was open on the table and I glanced at the page. "This is what you're using to deal with the flying monkeys?"

It isn't specific to the species, but I think it will do the trick.

I flipped to the green tab marked "locator spell." I'd added colored tabs to the book for quick references.

"Do we have all the ingredients? I need barberry bark, birch leaves, chickweed, and..."

I'm familiar with the list, miss. He fluttered to the cabinet and scanned the jars and labels, reading aloud. *Angelica root, arrowroot, barberry bark, birch leaves, cackleberries, catnip, chamomile flowers... .*

"Wait, back up. Did you say cackleberries?"

Yes, miss. The emergency rations.

I was a complete idiot. Of course, I had emergency rations. "After we finish the locator spell, I need you to whip up a batch of truth serum for me. Can I count on you?"

Always, miss. He finished reviewing the inventory. *It appears we have what we need for the locator spell as well. It isn't one we've had to concoct very often.*

That was true. In fact, the last time I'd used it was when Paul the toad didn't return home to Evian's for a whole weekend. She was convinced he'd been flattened by a golf cart or swallowed by a pelican. She was too distraught to cast the spell herself, so I volunteered. Turned out he was spending quality time with a lady toad in the forest and did *not* appreciate our inopportune interruption. Although I tried to use the incident as a learning opportunity for Evian to give Paul some space, it didn't stick. She was back to co-dependency inside of a week.

"Okay, let's get started." I spread the town map across the table and placed a penny in the middle.

I'll mix the ingredients, Gerald said.

"Make sure not to spill any," I said. "You know how hard it is to clean up those tiny pieces."

I'm quite aware, miss, as I generally perform such tasks.

"Thanks, Gerald," I said, when he'd finished. "I might actually make you bacon and eggs for the rest of the week."

My hands hovered over the mixture as I recited, "Searching high and low for the singer in my show. Don't let this be like pulling teeth. Move the penny and show me Keith." I felt the magic's warmth spread to my fingertips.

The penny is moving, miss, Gerald said.

Thank Goddess. I opened my eyes in time to see the penny stop over the location of the resort and spa.

"Fire up the scooter, Gerald," I said. "Looks like I have a diva to interrogate."

Chapter Twelve

Dylan sat behind the desk, reading a comic book, one of those male fantasy stories in which the superhero is impossibly built and his love interest has watermelons for boobs and a waist the size of my arm. Talk about wish fulfillment. When he saw me approaching, he slipped the comic book onto his lap, out of sight.

"Hey there, Kenna," he stammered. "Are you here for a treatment? I don't remember seeing your name on the schedule because I definitely would have noticed." He seemed to realize how stalkerish that sounded. "I mean, I always pay attention when important people in Eternal Springs have appointments here."

That was better. I offered him my most relaxed smile. I suspected it looked more as if I were asking him to check my teeth for lettuce after eating a salad.

"Not to worry. You haven't missed anything, Dylan. I'm not here for my appointment. I'm here for someone else's. Could you take a quick look and tell me which room Keith Simonson is in? He asked me to meet him here to talk about the Battle of the Bands competition."

Dylan shuffled papers around nervously. We both understood the situation. I was asking for confidential information and he wasn't supposed to give it to me. I'd already wrangled Mike Simpons's location out of him, but at least Mike had been there to fix the hot tub. Director of tourism or not, I wasn't entitled to guest information at the resort and spa. It seemed Dylan would take a bit more persuasion.

"Look, this was Keith's idea. I already know he's here, but I can't remember which room he said he'd be in. I promise I won't tell anyone that you told me," I said. "It'll be our little secret."

Dylan hesitated. "I don't know. I feel like every time I help one of you out, it ends up biting me on the nose."

I arched an eyebrow. "One of you?" I repeated. "What's that supposed to mean?"

His cheeks reddened. "You know, you St. Joan's graduates." He scratched the back of his neck. "Technically, I guess you didn't graduate from there. Anyway, you, Skye, Zola, and Evian. You always need information and I give it to you, then I get in trouble. That's the cycle."

I smiled demurely. "Some trouble is worth getting into, though, don't you think?"

Dylan frowned. "No. I like my job. I don't want any trouble."

I didn't have time for this. I should have just performed a glamour spell and disguised myself as Buddy. It would have saved me the hassle.

"Dylan, what if I make it worth your while? You tell me which room Keith is in and I'll...."

"Go for a ride with me on one of those tandem bicycles?" he asked eagerly.

That was not the response I was expecting. "You want to what?"

Dylan seemed to warm to his idea. "You know those bicycles with two seats and two sets of pedals. You can rent them from Wanda's Wheels."

I shook my head, confused. "Yes, of course I know Wanda's Wheels." You didn't become tourism director without knowing all of the available tourist activities. "If that's your request, I'll honor it."

"We'll ride along the coastal path on a bicycle built for two," he said happily.

Dylan was a strange kid, but a bike ride seemed to be a fair exchange. "Deal. Which room?" At this rate, Keith's treatment would be over if I didn't hurry.

"He's with Margo for a massage," Dylan said. "I'll let you know when I can rent the bike. The tandems are super popular."

I doubted that very much, but said, "Sounds good." I hurried down the corridor to Margo's room. I didn't bother to knock. I simply clicked open the door and crept inside. The interior of the room was dark, but I could see Keith's face down on the table, a towel covering his backside. Margo's fingers were kneading his shoulders.

"Who's that, Margo?" Keith asked sleepily. "I didn't ask for a friend today."

I shot Margo a quizzical look. This was not that kind of spa. Margo rolled her eyes.

"It doesn't matter how many times you do ask for a friend," Margo said, "it's never going to happen. Not here, anyway."

"But I'm a rockstar," Keith objected. "Haven't you heard the news? Fat Gandalf is going to win the Battle of the Bands and then we're going to take off like a rocket. You can say you did me when."

"I don't think your wife would appreciate anyone doing you except her," Margo said.

I sat on a leather stool in the corner of the room, next to

the oils and stones. The room smelled earthy like patchouli. Zola would have enjoyed the ambience. Personally, I preferred smells like cinnamon and cranberry.

"You know Rachel looks the other way," Keith said. "It's part of our arrangement."

"And does that arrangement work both ways?" I asked.

Keith's chin jerked up as he tried to identify the source of the voice. "I thought I heard someone come in. Do you always barge in on massages, Kenna?"

"It's part of my job," I lied. "I perform spot checks on the spa to make sure guests are happy. I didn't realize Margo was with a local. Sorry about that." But I still wanted him to answer my question.

"I don't mind you staring at my naked body if you don't," Keith said. He put his face back in the headrest.

I scowled. Keith was a piece of work. No wonder Rachel cheated on him with Pete. By all accounts, Pete was a nice guy. Keith seemed to be taking his role as lead singer far too seriously.

"So how about it?" I asked. "Is Rachel allowed to step outside the marriage as well? Seems only fair."

"Why would she feel the need to do that when she has me?" He turned his head to the side to look at me. "She's only taken advantage of her free pass only once, that I know of. We agreed not to tell each other, but that doesn't stop other people from talking about it."

I decided to take a chance. "So you knew about her and Pete?"

"Ooh, yeah. Right there, babe," he moaned, as Margo pressed harder. "Yeah, I knew. Tiffany was clueless, though. Still is, to the best of my knowledge. I hope it stays that way. No point in ruining her image of him now."

"Were you upset when you found out about it?" I asked.

"Even though you and Rachel had an agreement, I'm sure you didn't expect her to choose your bandmate."

Margo appeared surprisingly relaxed during the conversation. I had to imagine she'd heard worse conversations on the table.

"To be honest, it felt a little like crapping where you eat," he said. "I prefer to keep my extracurricular activities away from our day-to-day lives. For whatever reason, Rachel and Pete decided to take advantage of their relationship. She and I haven't talked about it, but I suspect it was more about convenience than anything else."

"And maybe it was a little bit that Rachel wanted to get back at you," I pressed. It seemed passive aggressive to target his drummer. If she was going to have an affair, she could have chosen the postman or any number of men not connected to Keith.

"I wasn't surprised by Rachel's choice," Keith said. "She can be a real shrew sometimes. It was Pete's decision to participate that kinda threw me for a loop."

"Did you ever speak to him about it?" I asked.

"No way," Keith said. "And if he'd ever brought it up, I would have pretended not to know. No good could come from acknowledging it."

"And are you still seeing other women?" I asked.

Keith raised his chin and stared at me. "Why? You interested? You might want to jump on the bandwagon now, before it gets too full." He craned his neck toward Margo. "You, too, Margo."

Margo now had a smooth stone in each hand, ready to rub them on his back. Like Keith and his women, I couldn't resist a good opportunity. I focused on the stones and said a little spell under my breath. Margo placed the stones on his back and stepped away for more oil. I continue to focus on the stones.

"Ouch! Get them off!" Keith apparently couldn't take the heat. He flipped onto his side, knocking the hot stones to the floor. "I told you before, Margo. I like them room temperature." He whimpered like a child.

Margo's brow creased. "They were, I swear. I never warmed them up."

He glanced over to the heater to see that it was turned off.

"Sometimes our skin is unusually sensitive during times of emotional strain," I said. "You're probably more upset about Pete's death than you realize."

"Of course I'm upset about Pete's death," Keith snapped. He flipped over on the table. "Our new drummer isn't half as good as Pete, but he's all we've got at this point. I want to win this competition. Pete would want that."

"How's Rachel handling his death?" I asked. If she'd been having an affair with Pete, she might be more upset than she was willing to admit. I had to imagine it was difficult for her, not able to fully express her grief without tipping off her husband.

"How should I know?" he asked. "That would require us to have an actual conversation. Rachel doesn't have conversations. She talks *at* you."

Sheesh. No wonder they had a semi-open marriage. It seemed like they couldn't stand each other.

"Well, I can see you're in good hands, so I'll move on to the next guest." I rose to my feet. "Sorry about the interruption."

"Next time you come in here when I'm naked, you'd better be naked, too," Keith said.

Ugh. Not a chance.

I gave Margo a sympathetic look before slipping out the door.

. . .

I stood in the kitchen, preparing bacon and eggs for Gerald for the rest of the week. I pondered my conversation with Keith as I scrambled the eggs. As much as I disliked Keith's attitude, I didn't think he was the killer. He seemed more upset about Pete's absence from the band than his wife's affair.

Stuart banged on the window with his beak. "Tut incoming!"

I crunched on an apple. "I have a doorbell, Stuart," I said, not that the hairless cat would be able to reach it. In fact, he generally found a way into my house without knocking—one of his unsettling tricks.

Sure enough, Tut emerged in the kitchen. "You might have the decency to keep a can of tuna handy in the event of visitors."

"I have bacon and eggs," I said, holding up the pan.

Gerald zipped around the corner. *I'm sure I can accommodate you. Give me a moment.*

"There's no time," Tut said. "I need Kenna to come to the forest. The flying monkeys are there now."

My teeth sank into the apple and stayed there. The flying monkeys were in the forest. Right now. I bit down and chewed slowly, trying to decide what to do. I hadn't managed to review Gerald's spell yet.

"Are they circling overhead or what?" I asked.

"They're tormenting the trees at the moment," Tut said. "The trees don't like it when the fruit's on the other branch."

"Is that like they can dish it out, but they can't take it?" I queried.

"Agatha is ready to uproot herself," Tut said. "She's quite distressed."

This, I'd like to see.

I hurried from the house and hopped on my scooter. I

started the engine before I even secured my helmet, something I never did.

Shouldn't we review the spell book first, miss? Gerald asked.

"These guys have wings, Gerald. I don't have time to monkey around." I hesitated. "No pun intended."

What will you do to them, miss? Gerald asked anxiously.

"No clue," I said. "I'll assess the situation when I get there."

The real question, though, was what would they do to me?

Tut led me to the Cottonmouth Copse, where the flying monkeys were tormenting the sarcastic trees. One of the monkeys was peeing on the base of a tree, while another one was hanging from a branch by his tail and pulling strips of bark off the trunk.

"Stop stripping me, you filthy animal," Agatha shouted.

"It's the serious dark-haired one, thank the gods," Myra said. "I've never been happier to see one of your kind in my life."

"Please, could you eject these wretched creatures from the forest?" Earl said. "They're destroying the copse."

The monkeys regarded me with interest.

"Her kind is a witch," the peeing winged monkey said.

"That's right," I said, stepping forward. "And this is my domain you're encroaching upon."

"Ooh, we're encroaching upon it, are we?" the hanging monkey said. He loosened his tail and hovered in the air beside the tree, his wings flapping at high speed like a dragonfly's.

"What are you gonna do about it?" the third monkey jeered, "knock us down when you flip your glossy hair over your shoulder?"

"Her hair *is* glossy," Earl agreed. "I've always admired the sheen. Do you use a special product to achieve that?"

"What are you doing here, foul beasts?" I demanded. "And what are your intentions?"

"I intend to carve out a nice piece of land for us," the peeing monkey said. He was clearly the leader of their trio. "Now that I've identified adequate food sources."

The way he said "food sources" made my skin crawl. "You mean fruit from the trees, right?"

"Hey!" Agatha objected. "That's assault."

"Fruit?" the alpha monkey snorted. "Hardly. We like meat."

"There's a wonderful deli downtown," I said. "They carry the best cured meats on the island."

The monkey's thick brow wrinkled. "We don't buy over the counter. We hunt."

I swallowed hard. "Hunt? I suppose there are plenty of worms and small woodland creatures... ."

"Puppies," the hovering monkey said. "We have a taste for puppies."

"Or small dogs," the third monkey said. "The age is unimportant. It's the size that matters."

"You don't hear that sentiment every day," Earl said. "Good on you for keeping an open mind like that."

I groaned.

"Shut up, Earl," Agatha said. "These flying monkeys are telling us they eat puppies. *Eat* them. Not play fetch."

Earl hesitated. "I see. That does present an issue, doesn't it? Puppies are cute."

"What's your position on kittens?" Tut asked.

The monkeys began spitting and making faces.

"Kittens are disgusting," the alpha monkey said. "We'd never touch them."

Tut appeared satisfied. "Carry on, then." He began to walk away.

"Are you kidding me?" I yelled. "You've been the one complaining about their poop all over the forest, but you're willing to walk away because they don't eat your babies?"

Tut shrugged his naked shoulders. "I have to choose my battles, Kenna, as do you." He padded into the forest and disappeared.

"What a nerve!" I couldn't believe it. I turned and faced the monkeys. "You need to go back to where you came from."

The monkeys chortled.

"There aren't any puppies there," the third monkey said. "Here is much better."

"No one's entitled to puppies," I said. "It's time to go home, fellas."

"And who's going to make us?" the alpha asked.

I gave them my most menacing stare. "I am."

My statement instigated more mocking laughter, followed by the worst attack I'd ever endured.

Splat!

Slowly, my gaze shifted to my crisp, white shirt. A brown stain stared back at me, from the left side of my chest. It was worse than any prank Skye had ever pulled. My temper flared.

"Do you know how expensive dry cleaning is on an island?" I asked through clenched teeth.

"Send me the bill," the hovering monkey said, "so I can use it as toilet paper."

The monkeys roared with laughter again.

"We're more fun than a barrel of us," the third monkey chortled.

I rolled up my sleeves. Enough was enough. I couldn't risk starting a forest fire, so I had to think of something else. I thought back to the basic spells we learned in school, before the coven's unfortunate evacuation. Under pressure, the only one coming to mind was one we used for pranks on each other.

I waved my hand in the air and chanted, "I pity you for engaging a witch, best of luck trying to scratch this itch." I felt the energy rise within me and shoot from my fingertips.

The flying monkeys immediately began clawing at their bodies, too uncomfortable to remain still. It wasn't enough to send them back to the other dimension, but it would have to do for now.

"Scratch my back and I'll scratch yours," the alpha commanded. The other two were too busy dealing with their own itching bodies. All three were too preoccupied to take to the skies.

"Everywhere itches," the third monkey complained. "I can't reach the tips of my wings."

As satisfying as it was to watch them squirm, I needed to get out of there. Now that I knew puppies were at risk, I had to take more drastic action. And soon.

"'Til we meet again," I called over my shoulder. I hopped on my scooter and sped away.

Chapter Thirteen

Tonight was the night to pay the piper or, in this case, Skye. I sat at a table at Coconuts on Friday night for the dreaded karaoke. To my dismay, it seemed that every band in town for the competition had heard about karaoke night and decided it was a good opportunity to show off. I had no doubt that Skye had spread the word in order to get as many people here as possible to witness my humiliation.

Thankfully, Bonnie Fisher was behind the bar tonight, which would go a long way toward a smooth evening. I watched her prepare a couple of pitchers of rum runners and quickly realized they were headed for our table. My gaze darted to Skye, who sat across from Zola and Evian. I had no doubt this was her doing. She probably wanted me to get good and drunk before she made me sing my song. That witch would do anything to torture me.

I bit the bullet and strode to the table.

"You haven't held up your end of the bargain," Skye accused, when she noticed me. "Showing up doesn't count."

"It's not my fault if the rockstars are hogging the microphone," I said.

"You don't have to worry," she replied. "I added your name to the list half an hour ago. You'll get your turn."

I stuck out my tongue. Skye knew how to get under my skin better than anyone else. She was like the annoying sister I never wanted.

"Then what are you worried about?" I asked. "I'll keep my end of the deal."

"Not completely," Skye said. She made a big show of scanning the bar area. "I don't see Skywalker here, do you?"

My stomach sank. On the one hand, I was relieved not to sing in front of him. On the other hand, I worried that Skye would make good on her threat to publish the story before I was ready. I couldn't decide which was worse.

"Hold onto your lightsabers, ladies," Zola said. "Here comes Skywalker now."

My pulse quickened at the sight of him. He loped across the bar. He had such a confident, casual air about him that you couldn't help but be drawn to him.

"Someone's gone dreamy eyed," Evian announced.

Skye immediately began to fill our glasses with rum runners from a pitcher, starting with mine.

"Drink up, Obi-Tense Kenobi," Skye snickered.

"Please don't make a big deal about him," I pleaded quietly. That was exactly the wrong thing to say. Immediately, my witchy sisters began calling his name and motioning for him to join us. I slumped in my seat, bracing for the fallout.

"I haven't missed you, have I?" Lucas asked. He looked even better up close. He wore a hot pink polo shirt and jeans. Any guy who could pull off a shirt like that was a guy worth ogling. He sat down in the empty chair beside me.

"You haven't missed much," I said. "All the bands on the island seem to have come out to get their cover song on tonight," I said. "If I hear Dream On one more time, I'll drown myself in rum runners."

Lucas nodded toward the pitchers. "It looks like you're about to do that anyway."

"Liquid courage," I said. "I'm not exactly excited by the prospect of getting up there."

Lucas squinted. "Really? You always seem to have so much confidence. I guess I'm surprised to hear that you're nervous about something."

"That's not the only thing she's nervous about tonight," Skye muttered under her breath. I kicked her under the table and felt satisfied to see her wince.

"Lucas, I don't know if you remember them from high school, but this is Skye, and that's Zola and Evian."

Zola raised her drink and Evian waved.

"I think it's nice that the four of you are still friends after all these years," he said. "I don't really keep in touch with many people from high school."

The four of us exchanged glances. Our entangled relationships weren't necessarily by choice. Then again, we always seemed to end up spending time with each other, so maybe our distaste for one another was more bluster than anything else.

"You'd better drink up, Kenna," Evian said. "Your number has to be soon."

I downed my drink and poured another one. I wanted to do whatever was necessary to block this night from my memory. One look at Lucas however, made me question my plan. I didn't want to forget how good he looked tonight. Maybe it would be worth staying sober just for that. My gaze traveled over his shoulder to the table behind us. Keith Simonson sat with his bandmates and his wife, Rachel. They looked like they'd sailed past Tipsy Town and were headed straight for Obliterationville. Keith's eyes were bloodshot and

Rachel swayed gently from side to side, as though a strong gust of wind might blow her over. I realized this might be a good chance to speak to her about Pete because her defenses were clearly down. When Keith was called up to the stage for his cover song, I seized the chance.

"I'll be right back," I said, and took my drink with me. I didn't trust Skye alone with my drink. Knowing her, she'd either lick the ice cubes and put them back in or cast a spell on the rum runner. I was already going to make a fool of myself tonight. I didn't need her magical assistance.

Then I recognized the opening cords of Dream On.

"Sweet Goddess above," I muttered. "I'm not listening to that one again."

Keith swaggered across the stage as though he were Mick Jagger incarnate. I remembered his attitude at the spa and felt my blood pressure rise. Now was the perfect opportunity for revenge on behalf of all women. I wouldn't be able to cast a complicated spell quickly, but I could certainly make things interesting.

As discreetly as I could, I wiggled my fingers and chanted, "When the working day is done, girls like Keith just want to have fun."

I sank into the chair beside Rachel and smiled as the Cyndi Lauper song began.

"What's he singing?" Rachel asked. I noticed her slurred speech.

"Sounds like he's a fan of '80s music," I said, "which is completely understandable, because it's awesome." My spirits rose as he danced around the stage, belting out *Girls Just Wanna Have Fun*. He looked and sounded ridiculous, and the crowd ate it up.

"Leave it to my husband to turn an emasculating moment into a chance for more adoration," Rachel said bitterly. She barely seemed to register my presence next to her.

I sipped my rum runner. "How are you holding up, Rachel? I imagine you're all processing Pete's death."

Rachel's expression hardened. Hmm. Maybe drunkenness wouldn't be enough to break through her defenses. Good thing I had the cackleberry truth serum on hand, thanks to Gerald and my emergency rations.

"What are you drinking, Rachel?" I asked. "It looks delicious."

"'S called a filthy witch," she said, nodding to the table top. Well, that seemed appropriate.

"I think I'll try one," I said. "I'll get you one, as well."

Rachel nodded, her attention fixed on her husband. Keith was still hopping around the stage like an adolescent girl. I hurried to Bonnie. There was no time to waste. I ordered the drinks and poured the truth serum from the vial in my pocket. I made sure to note which hand Rachel's glass was in. I wasn't about to risk casting a spell on myself.

I returned to the table with the drinks and handed Rachel the one in my left hand.

"Sanks," she slurred. She gulped it down as if it was water. "You sure this was a filthy witch? Tastes like berry."

I gulped mine. "I don't taste berries in mine." I waited for a moment for the spell to take effect. Keith's song was ending, so I cast another quick spell to keep him on the stage. Tiffany's *I Think We're Alone Now* would do the trick.

"Did Keith know about your relationship with Pete?" I asked. Since I knew the answer was yes, so if she said no, I would know the serum hadn't kicked in yet.

"A course," Rachel wobbled. "I made sure he knew. I wasn't gonna let him be the only one out there having fun."

"What about Tiffany?" I probed. "Did she know?"

Rachel made a face. "She's got her head stuck too far into that welder's mask to notice anything about Pete. All she cares about is her business. Pete just wanted to have fun once in a while." A faint smile touched her lips. "Like Cyndi Lauper."

"And did you?" I asked. "Have fun together?"

Rachel smirked. "Oh, we did. As often as the opportunity presented itself."

"Did you love him?"

Rachel recoiled. "Love him? Don't be absurd. I used Pete for sex. My husband's swagger only extends to the stage. It doesn't quite make it to the bedroom, if you know what I mean."

Oh. I guess it didn't surprise me that Keith was overcompensating with his persona. It wouldn't be the first time that a man put on airs for the sake of his ego.

"But what about all these women he claims to sleep with?" I asked. "If he's that disappointing, wouldn't word get around?"

Rachel shrugged. "You'd be surprised what women put up with." She eyed me carefully. "Or maybe you wouldn't be surprised. Anyway, Keith is the lead singer in a band. It doesn't matter whether they're famous or not. There are plenty of women out there who want to say that they slept with him. Keith takes full advantage of that."

"So I guess that means you didn't intend to leave Keith for Pete," I said.

"'Solutely not," Rachel scoffed, "specially not when his star is on the rise. Pete didn't want to leave Tiffany, either. He begged her to go on tour if and when Fat Gandalf headed to the mainland, but she refused."

Well, that fit with what Tiffany had told me.

"Do you think you and Pete would've continued your affair on the road?" I asked.

"I assume so," Rachel replied. "I guess we'll never know, will we?"

Keith's song ended and the bar erupted in applause. He

took a deep bow and nearly fell off the stage in a drunken stupor. I certainly hoped he was better behaved for the Battle of the Bands competition.

"Oh, look," Rachel said. "What a surprise. Lizzie's going to sing."

"Lizzie?" I echoed. "Pete's sister-in-law?"

Rachel nodded. "I guess Mike is watching the kids for a change. About time. That woman's like a caged animal."

Lizzie took the microphone and busted out a Pat Benatar song like a professional diva. "She's amazing," I said. "She's not in a band?"

"How could she be?" Rachel asked. "With Pete busy with the band, Mike works triple time. Lizzie has no choice but to look after the kids and do little else."

I thought Lizzie's decision to sing Pat Benatar at Coconuts so soon after her brother's death was odd. Then again, Pete's bandmates and his lover were also here, so maybe that was how the musically-inclined handled grief. I wasn't one to judge.

Lizzie finished her song to wild applause.

"To the manor born," Rachel muttered.

Someone tapped me on the shoulder. "They called your name, Kenna." I whipped around to see Skye grinning.

Rachel looked shocked. "You're singing?"

"Not by choice," I replied.

"I didn't think so," Rachel said. "You seem far too uptight to be a performer."

Skye bit back a smile. "Let's go, Byrne."

"Fine," I huffed. "No need to manhandle me. I'm going." So not only did I need to sing, but I needed to follow a very talented Lizzie. Great.

I made my way to the stage, feeling the heat burn the back of my neck. Buddy had no idea the lengths I would go to in order to protect the island's reputation. If he thought somebody else could do a better job, he was kidding himself.

I cringed when I realized which song Skye had chosen for me. She didn't even give me the courtesy of a power ballad. Instead, it was *When Doves Cry* by Prince. I couldn't sing in A minor. What was Skye thinking?

I had no choice but to give it my best.

The song was far too sexy for me. I warbled and prayed for the torture to end quickly. My hair suddenly blew back as if I were in a Whitesnake video and I knew Skye was responsible for that special effect.

The only applause came from my table. I couldn't bear to look at Lucas.

"Teamwork makes the dream work," I said, when I returned to the table.

Skye rolled her eyes and groaned. "If I hear you say that one more time, I'm going to make you sing an encore."

"That was a fine performance, Miss Byrne," Lucas said.

"It was awful, but I appreciate the sentiment, Mr. Skywalker…I mean…" *Crap.*

Lucas grinned. "Talk about a high school flashback."

"Sorry," I mumbled. I was sure my cheeks flamed crimson.

He extended his hand. "Now that I know you can sing, maybe you could impress me with your dancing skills."

I didn't know that *impress* was the right word. *Horrify* was probably more appropriate.

The woman onstage began to croon Madonna's *Crazy For You*.

"What do you know?" Lucas said. "Time to slow things down. You could probably use the break."

"What does that mean?" I asked, as we joined the other dancers.

"Like I said before—you're always on the go." He pulled

me closer and began to sway to the beat. "Slow down with me."

"I...I can't," I said. "There's always so much to do." Like solve a murder. Run a successful Battle of the Bands competition. Capture flying monkeys. The list was endless...and tiring. My body began to relax in his arms. Great Goddess, he was built like a refrigerator. A soft, comfy refrigerator.

"That's better, isn't it?" he whispered in my ear.

It was. The rest of the bar faded away as I danced in his arms. "Now you can demonstrate how Pete and Rachel were making out," I murmured. Wait, what did I just say? I clamped my hand over my mouth.

Lucas pulled back slightly. "What was that? I couldn't hear you over the music."

"I said Rachel's here." I tilted my head toward her table. "The one who had the affair with Pete."

Lucas followed my gaze to Fat Gandalf's table. "They all look pretty sloshed."

"Could someone get me a waffle with whipped cream?" a voice called.

My radar pinged. Waffle? "Is the Waffle Wagon here?"

"It's out front," another voice said. "You'd better hurry."

Of course it was. Now I was torn between continuing to enjoy the feel of Lucas's strong arms or the capture of my white waffle whale. Life was so ridiculously unfair.

I looked up at Lucas and got momentarily lost in those bright blue eyes...until someone walked by with a liege Belgian waffle.

"Would you excuse me for a second?" I said. As hard as it was to tear myself away, I had to make a run for the Waffle Wagon. I couldn't let a man come between me and my goal, even one as staggeringly handsome as Lucas Holmes.

I made a beeline for the front of Coconuts and began

swearing like a vampire pirate as I watched darkness swallow the red wagon at the end of the street.

"Kenna?"

I spun around to see Lucas. "Sorry about that. I don't usually talk like that." Only after several rum runners and a filthy witch.

He laughed. "It doesn't offend me." He moved closer. "In fact, I kinda like it." He peered into he darkness. "What made you run out here?"

I sighed. No point in hiding the truth. "I was making a run for the Waffle Wagon."

"You were craving a Belgian waffle?"

I explained my endless pursuit of the Wagon Waffle.

"It's like Charlie Brown and the football," he said.

"Sort of." I preferred my Moby Dick comparison, but who was I to quibble over cultural references?

He placed an arm around my shoulders and squeezed. "You're a fighter, Kenna. I have no doubt that one day soon you'll triumph over the Waffle Wagon."

"I'm glad you have that kind of faith in me."

"How could I not? You're a force of nature, Kenna Byrne."

Oh, he had no idea.

Chapter Fourteen

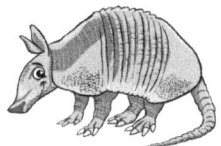

I awoke to the sound of knocking. I rolled over and pulled a pillow over my head to muffle the noise. My head pounded from too many drinks at Coconuts and all I wanted to do was sleep. After all, it was Saturday, and I deserved a couple extra hours of rest.

Someone's here, miss, Gerald announced, fluttering beside the bed.

"I'm aware of that, thank you," I mumbled.

Do you want me to see who it is? he asked.

"That would be nice." I kept the pillow pressed over my face. As long as I could still breathe, that was the important thing.

Gerald returned twenty seconds later. *It's Dottie.*

Dottie? At my house on a Saturday? That didn't bode well. I forced myself out of bed and padded down the hall to the stairs. There was no time to make myself presentable. Bed hair and a Wonder Woman T-shirt with leggings would have to do.

Dottie pursed her lips at my appearance. "Was there a home invasion last night?"

"More like a head invasion," I said. "Too much alcohol in one sitting." I drew back to let her pass.

"That's the reason I'm here."

"You're here because I drank too much?" Dottie was motherly, but she wasn't *that* motherly.

"No, because a few of the band members drank too much and apparently sang themselves hoarse after one too many Debbie Gibson songs."

"Hoarse?" My stomach knotted. "Are you telling me we're losing participants in the competition?"

"Not yet," Dottie said. "But they want you to rework the schedule so their voices have more time to recover."

I closed my eyes and prayed to the Goddess for strength. "How many are we talking about?" I'd slaved over that schedule and now I'd have to undo all my hard work. I inhaled deeply and tried to calm my nerves. I had no one to blame but myself. After all, I cast the spell on Keith and kicked off a trend. The response to his performance was so positive that every other band member felt the need to follow suit.

"Tell me which bands," I said. I went to the small antique secretary against the wall and grabbed a notepad and a pen.

Dottie reeled off a few names. "I'm sorry to be the bearer of bad news," she said, once she'd finished. "I know how hard you work and how little Buddy appreciates it."

"Good thing I don't do it for Buddy," I said. I forced a smile. "Can I offer you a drink? I have that mixed berry tea you like."

"No, thanks," she said. "I'm off to beach yoga. I only wanted to swing by and give you the heads up as soon as possible. I know how you like to plan."

"That I do." I walked Dottie to the door and waved goodbye, already reconfiguring the competition schedule in my head. It was like reworking the pieces of a mental puzzle.

Dottie was barely out of view when I noticed a familiar set of broad shoulders jogging my way.

"Skywalker, incoming!" Stuart yelled.

My jaw clenched as my headache worsened. It was like Athena was threatening to spring from my head in a suit of armor.

"Thank you, Stuart. You can go now."

"What if you need my assistance?" the albino raven asked.

"I feel comfortable letting you go."

"There's something else..." Stuart began, but I cut him off with a stern look. Lucas was nearly here and I couldn't risk him catching me deep in conversation with a bird. He already thought I was a waffle-chasing lunatic.

"You're up," Lucas said cheerfully. "I wasn't sure what to expect." He slowed when he saw my appearance. "I guess that *is* what I expected."

"Hey!" I objected. "Where's Leia and why are you wearing a shirt?"

He smirked. "Is that a complaint? Because I can take this one off. It did get a little sweaty on the walk over."

"No, no." I waved my hands. "I just wondered if you were out for a jog."

"Not right now. I came straight from the airfield."

"Straight here? Why?"

He gestured to the door. "Can I come in or do you require gentleman callers to remain on the front porch?"

I cringed. I was the director of tourism for an entire island and I didn't know how to be polite to the only guy I was attracted to. "I'm sorry. Come in. Can I get you a drink? I'm going to make myself a cup of tea."

"Iced tea, maybe? The weather's warmer than I expected."

"Yeah, you make me hot just looking at you." My whole body tensed when I realized what I said. There wasn't enough magic in the world to lessen my horror. I tried again—

"Because you look so hot." Goddess have mercy, what was wrong with me?

Lucas chuckled. "I get the idea. I look like a sweaty mess." He promptly removed his shirt. "Is that better?"

Wow! So much better. "Let me get that drink for you." I hurried to the fridge before I said anything stupid and pulled out a pitcher of iced tea. I brought two glasses back to the living room.

"I thought you were making yourself hot tea," Lucas said.

"I needed to cool down." I took a long sip. "So why did you need to come here from the airfield?"

"You'll never guess who flew in from the mainland this morning," he said.

"Bruce Springsteen?"

He gave me an amused look. "Someone more relevant to the current situation."

"Sherlock Holmes?"

"Let me help you out because your brain function is clearly compromised. Barb Simpson, Pete's mother." He gulped down the rest of his iced tea.

"She's here for the funeral, I guess."

Lucas nodded. "And Lizzie was at the airfield to pick her up with all three kids in tow."

"Poor Lizzie. She looked drunk as a skunk by the end of the night."

"And she looked worse than you this morning," Lucas said. "One night of drinking must've hit her pretty hard."

"Gee, thanks. Where was Mike?"

"Working," Lucas said. "Apparently, he was supposed to pick her up, but got called to a job. Lizzie did not look pleased about it. I'm pretty sure I saw steam coming out of her ears."

"I guess so with a hangover and three kids to care for," I replied.

"I could hear complaining the whole way to the golf cart with Pete's mom. The poor woman just flew in for her son's funeral."

"I can only imagine how Lizzie would have handled Pete's decision to tour with Fat Gandalf." I paused, the gears of my mind clicking away. Maybe Pete's death *was* how Lizzie chose to handle his decision.

"I feel horrible for the whole family," Lucas said. "It has to be a sad and confusing time for them."

I studied Lucas's expression. He was much more compassionate than I'd ever been. I was accustomed to the tough love of Skye and the other witches. Lucas didn't seem to have a snarky bone in his sculpted body.

"Lucas," I said slowly. "There's something I've been meaning to tell you."

His blue eyes twinkled. "Go away, creeper?"

"Not quite." *Definitely not*. I sucked in a breath. "In high school, do you remember the Darth Vader pranks?"

He frowned. "You mean the photos of Darth Vader that had 'I am your father' written on them?"

"Yes, those."

"How could I forget? They were in my locker, on my book covers, even in the toilet stall. They popped everywhere I went, as if by magic."

I pressed my lips together. It was now or never. "I hate to tell you this, but my friends and I—the ones you met last night—were responsible and I'm really sorry. It was only meant as a harmless prank."

Lucas gaped at me in disbelief. "*You* did that?"

I nodded. "We'd seen you in the forest one day, practicing with your lightsaber..." I couldn't finish. There was no justification for our behavior. We were mean girls, plain and simple.

Lucas flinched as though I'd hit him. "The other kids

mocked me mercilessly. That's why they started calling me Skywalker."

"I know. I'm so sorry. You have no idea."

He set the empty glass down on the coffee table and I resisted the urge to grab a coaster. Now didn't seem the right time.

"I thought you were special, Kenna," he said quietly. "I think I might have been mistaken."

He pulled his shirt back over his head and stalked out of the house without another word. I stared after him, unable to speak.

Confession is good for the soul, miss, Gerald said.

"I sure hope so," I said, "because it sucks for my love life."

TWO POWER BALLADS AND A SHOWER LATER, GERALD AND I sat in the secret room, considering options for dealing with the flying monkeys. I wanted a permanent solution, not the itching spell that probably only served to aggravate them. I also needed a spell that wouldn't attract too much attention. I'd been lucky so far that they'd managed to stay out of sight of the local population and away from innocent puppies. That luck was bound to run out soon if I didn't act.

"You need to be mindful of the spell's requirements," I said, when Gerald suggested a spell involving cages made of lava. He wanted to use them to transport the monkeys back to their hellhole.

But lava is one of your specialties, miss.

"That doesn't mean I have to use it."

Gerald paused, his gaze riveted to the spell book. *Need I point out that the Incident That Shall Not Be Named took place thirteen years ago, miss? You've grown up quite a bit since then.*

"What are you trying to say, Gerald?"

I think you may be avoiding certain options out of fear.

"I'm not afraid of my own powers," I objected.

I don't simply mean your powers, miss. I've noticed other instances—Lucas, flying, your need for order, your drive to succeed. They're all coping mechanisms driven by fear.

"Since when did you take on the role of therapist?" I snapped.

I read more than spell books and cookbooks in my spare time, Gerald said.

"I'm not using any major magic and that's final," I said. "I can't risk burning down the entire forest to get rid of three flying monkeys."

As you wish, miss, Gerald said.

"And I'm not afraid of anything," I said, "except mice." Which is completely understandable because mice are disgusting.

You're quite right, miss. I apologize for the suggestion.

I scanned the spell book for ideas that didn't involve fire. It was one thing to perform little spells like warming stones and hot tubs—those didn't have potential for mass destruction.

"Here's one that freezes them," I said, tapping the page. "If we stop them from moving, we can easily send them back to their dimension."

A freeze spell seems better suited to Evian, does it not?

"You're right." I sighed and flipped to the next page.

Perhaps it wouldn't be the worst thing in the world to enlist the aid of your coven sisters.

"I said I would take care of it and I will," I insisted.

I have no doubt, miss. Shall I prepare a pot of tea?

"That would be nice, thank you."

Gerald fluttered out of the secret room, his back end smacking the floor the whole way to the kitchen. I decided to look through the index to see if something jumped out at me. The spell to send the monkeys back wasn't the difficult part

—the difficult part was capturing them first in order to cast the spell. I sat cross-legged on the floor with the book on my lap, immersing myself in the possibilities. They had two distinct advantages over me—there were three of them and they could fly. But I knew I had the biggest advantage of all.

I was Kenna Byrne, overachiever extraordinaire. No demonic monkey in the world could compete with that.

THE TOWN CROAKER ISN'T FAR FROM MY OFFICE, SO I decided to pop in unannounced and make sure Skye wasn't secretly planning to renege on our deal now that my karaoke end of the bargain had been fulfilled. It wasn't that I didn't trust her…Okay, I totally didn't trust her.

As I walked through the front door, I noticed a man setting up a water cooler in the reception area. I wasn't sure why Skye bothered because she was the only one who worked there. Then I heard the distinct sound of flatulence. The water cooler man shot me a quizzical look, then immediately averted his gaze. There was only one witch with the power to move air that masqueraded as passing gas.

I cleared my throat and tried to regain my dignity. "Come out, come out, wherever you are, Skye."

She stepped out from behind her office door. The satisfied grin on her face told me what I needed to know.

"Very funny," I muttered, as I steered her back into the office by the elbow.

"To what do I owe such an honor?" Skye asked. "It isn't every day the esteemed director of island tourism comes to visit the lowly newspaper."

"I'm blocking out all sarcasm," I said.

She dropped into the chair behind her desk and spun around. "Then I don't know how you'll manage to understand a word I say."

I fought the urge to pinch her arm the way I did when we were younger. We were adults now, and physical torture was beneath us. Most of the time.

"You're sticking to your promise, right?" I asked pointedly.

Skye fluttered her eyelashes, all mock innocence. "Promise? What promise?"

I reached across the desk and squeezed the loose skin on the back of her bicep. Hard.

"Goddess of mercy, stop," Skye said, her breath catching.

I released her and she rubbed the sore spot on her arm. "I warned you."

"You're evil when you want to be," she grumbled.

My temper was much worse when we were younger. By all accounts, I'd chilled out significantly the past few years. My sister witches' arms were thankful for the change. I used to threaten to brand them with my initials.

"I'm not exactly having an easy week, Skye," I said. "So I need to make sure you're not going to throw me under the broomstick."

She held up her hands. "I won't. Really. In fact, I'll even share information with you."

I gave her a suspicious look. "Why would you do that?" Skye rarely shared intel. She hoarded it the way dragons hoarded treasure. I had been impressed that I'd managed to extract the information about Kyle Charney from her.

"Because I hate when you're stressed," she said. "It's a danger to public safety."

I folded my arms. "That's not true and you know it. I'd never let my magic hurt anyone." I'd never share with Skye the content of Gerald's recent thoughts regarding my fears. My familiar displayed far more compassionate than Skye could ever demonstrate.

"Not on purpose," Skye said.

When I lifted my hand to pinch her again, she rolled her chair out of reach.

"Don't make me do something I'd regret," I warned.

"Fine," Skye huffed. "Not that I think for a second you'd actually regret it." She adjusted her shirt. "There was an issue with the drummer's toxicology report, so Buddy has ordered that there be no investigation until another report can be performed."

"An issue?" I echoed. "What kind of issue?" It had already taken far longer than it should have to get the report. Then again, we all knew Abigail Marley was more interested in making money from plastic surgery than serving the public interest. In her mind, "beautifying" people by pumping them full of Botox *was* serving the public interest.

"Apparently, some clumsy idiot spilled Diet Coke on the initial results before anyone could review them." Skye stifled a laugh. "Abigail thinks all musicians are alcohol and drug addicts, so she and Buddy are convinced that the death was an accidental overdose and that the guy hit his head on the toilet seat and died."

Well, it was no surprise they agreed on that. "So Buddy still hasn't ordered an investigation," I said.

"Nope. Nor will he. He doesn't want to spend the money unless someone forces his hand."

I always knew Buddy was a tightwad, but this was ridiculous. I'd have to keep questioning people behind the scenes then.

"We can't have a killer running around loose," I said. "We have no idea why Pete was targeted. What if they attack someone else at the Battle of the Bands?"

"I think that's Buddy's other motive," Skye said. "He knows the town has spent a lot of money on the event. He wants everyone to believe it was an isolated incident, that the drummer brought it on himself. That way no one panics and the event goes off without a hitch."

"Believe me, I want the event to go smoothly more than anyone, but we can't pretend there isn't a killer running free," I said. "There's zero evidence that Pete was high that morning. The bag of pot was unopened and no one saw him acting loopy. I don't even know when he would have had time to smoke weed. He was too busy shuttling between Two Brothers and the band."

"And too busy dividing his time between his wife and his mistress, from what I hear," Skye added.

I pressed my lips together. "Please don't print that, Skye. You're not The National Enquirer."

"If I were The National Enquirer, I'd be writing that aliens impregnated Pete and he died in childbirth after spawning a tentacled baby with two heads, which went on to be adopted by Angelina Jolie."

I ignored her. "Pete's wife, Tiffany, doesn't know about Pete and Rachel. The woman just lost her husband. Do you really want to be the one to crush her world even more? Their marriage wasn't perfect, but she seemed to love him."

Skye played with a loose strand of her blond hair. "Quit the crybaby act. I told you I'd hold off on the story and I will. Like I said before, right now there's nothing to report." She shook a finger at me. "But I've been sharing with you, so if you learn something important, promise you'll tell me first."

"Promise," I said, and started for the door.

"Oh, before I forget...any leads on the flying monkeys?" she asked.

My blood ran cold and I whirled around. "What?"

"The monkeys." Skye pointed upward. "Hairy creatures with wings, soaring above the treetops and pooping wherever they please."

I leaned against the door. "How do you know about them? Have you seen them?"

"Not personally, but it's only a matter of time before people do. There was a report on a missing dog yesterday. Mrs. Abernathy's poodle, Mr. Chucklehead."

My hand flew to cover my mouth. "They flew off with a poodle?"

"Mrs. Abernathy described them as overfed bumblebees. Apparently, bumblebees are known for being hairy. Luckily for us, Mrs. Abernathy's known in the neighborhood for her dementia. The neighbors say she's usually searching for King Tut's tomb or the Golden Fleece."

At least she sounded adventurous. "What about Mr. Chucklehead?" I'd have to start forbidding Gerald to leave the house until the situation was resolved.

"He was found on the edge of the forest, unharmed," Skye said, and I released the breath I'd been holding. "She'd accidentally bathed him in her conditioner that morning. The story is that the poodle's fur was so silky, whatever flew off with him couldn't maintain a firm grip and gave up."

"And I suppose you went to investigate," I said.

"Paid a little visit to the Cottonmouth Copse."

More like the Bigmouth Copse. "I'll take care of the overfed bees," I said. "Just keep it to yourself, please."

"You're going to owe a lot of favors after this week, Kenna," she said, practically giddy.

"You and I are square," I said. "And don't you forget it."

"I never promised you anything about flying monkeys."

I pointed my finger at the light switch and zapped it, knocking out the electricity in the room. "Oops. Looks like you need to call an electrician. Too bad Mike is so busy these days."

I opened the door and sauntered out of the office.

Chapter Fifteen

With the competition days away and the murder unsolved, I was entering full stress mode. I rode my scooter over to HEX 66.6 to go over the station's coverage of the event in light of my schedule changes. Evian needed a list of the revised order and I wanted to see if she'd heard any gossip about Pete's death.

I tracked down Evian in the break room, painting her nails. She glanced up in surprise. "Congrats. You survived karaoke."

"Barely," I said.

"What brings you here? Shouldn't you be busy lining up the instruments by size?"

"Hardy har," I replied. Although now that she mentioned it, that wasn't such a bad idea. "I need to go over the schedule for the competition with you one more time to reflect recent changes."

Evian arched an eyebrow. "More schedule changes? That doesn't sound like you, Kenna."

I plopped in the chair across from her. "This has been

more challenging than I thought. So many bands. Pete's murder. The flying monkeys."

Evian snapped to attention. "They're still out there?"

Oops. I meant to keep that tidbit to myself. "They are, but not for much longer. Gerald and I have a plan."

"You'd better. If you need our help, you can admit it." She twisted the lid back on the polish and blew gently across her nails. "Asking for help doesn't make you weak."

"It isn't that." Okay, maybe it was a little bit. "It's that I know what your help means--an opportunity to wreak more havoc in my life."

Evian considered the accusation. "It *is* fun to torment you, but if there's a flying monkey problem, we should deal with it together. It impacts everyone."

I fidgeted with the stapler on the table. "I guess so, but I have this ingrained sense of responsibility. I saw the monkeys first and I said I'd handle them, therefore, they're my problem."

Evian regarded me carefully. "Are you sure it's not more than that?"

"What do you mean?" The stapler skipped out of my hand and clunked onto the floor. I slunk down to retrieve it, mildly embarrassed.

"The school burned down," Evian said. "*Burned*, Kenna. I'm sure the fact that fire was to blame has plagued you now and again."

"Now you sound like Gerald," I said. "I know it wasn't my fault." Mostly.

"The hellhole specializes in flames," Evian said, "plus there were other fire witches there at the time. The whole coven was still on the island then."

"True, but they weren't on watch that night. We were."

I met Evian's penetrating gaze. I didn't want to explore

this particular slice of history right now. I had more important matters to attend to.

"I'll take care of the airborne poop flingers," I said. "You focus on the broadcast. That's where I need your help."

Evian gave me a sympathetic smile. "I know it goes against your nature, but it's not your job to control every outcome of every situation. Let us help."

"As I said, you'll help me by revising the schedule for the competition." I pulled my planner from my bag. "Here are the tweaks I need..."

We were about to wrap up the discussion when a familiar voice interrupted.

"Kenna Byrne, you are a hard woman to track down." Rachel Simonson appeared in the doorway. "Your assistant—the one with the questionable fashion choices—she thought you might be here."

Evian looked at me, knitting her eyebrows. "Assistant?"

"Dottie," I said.

"She certainly is." Rachel's gaze shifted to the table. "Perfect! Your planner's already out. Let's talk." She took the seat beside me and whipped out her matching day planner.

Evian looked from mine to hers, her mouth twitching. "How interesting."

"Rachel, this is Evian, the owner of the station. Evian, this is Rachel Simonson. She's married to Keith, the lead singer for Fat Gandalf."

Rachel's mouth formed a thin line. "I'm also the *manager* for Fat Gandalf, which is the reason I'm here." She gave me a sharp look. "As a woman, I'd think you'd make an effort not to reduce me to the label of someone's wife."

Ouch. "I'm sorry, Rachel. You're absolutely right."

"While I'm here," Rachel turned to Evian, "maybe you could think about adding more of Fat Gandalf's songs to the local playlist. I don't hear us nearly enough considering how good we are."

Evian tried to temper her response. I knew firsthand that she didn't like anyone giving her orders when it came to her radio station. "I'll take it under advisement."

Rachel flipped open her book. "I'm not happy about the new lineup, Kenna, and I'd like to have it changed."

Across the table, Evian rolled her eyes. We'd only just finished reviewing the new schedule.

"I moved you to fifth to give the band time to ease into the competition," I said. I figured any extra time they had to recover after Pete's death would only serve to help them.

"No, that won't do at all," Rachel said. "I need them third or sooner."

"Third," I repeated. I scanned the schedule to see if I could manage the change easily. Who was I kidding? There was nothing easy about it. Still, I knew the band was reeling from Pete's death and I didn't want to make things harder for them. "For Pete's sake, I'll make it happen."

Rachel heaved a sigh of relief. "Thank you. Between the funeral and practice sessions, this week has been an absolute bear."

"How was the funeral?" I asked.

Rachel pulled a face. "Perfectly nice except for Lizzie's insistence on singing. She can't stand to be out of the spotlight for more than two seconds."

I tried to be diplomatic. "Well, people often sing at funerals."

Rachel's brow lifted, challenging me. "Do they often sing Shania Twain's *I Feel Like A Woman*? So incredibly tacky."

Hmm. Probably not. "Everyone expresses grief differently." That was my mantra and I was sticking to it.

"The only thing Lizzie was expressing was oxygen," Rachel said.

"Technically, that would be carbon dioxide," I said.

Evian stifled a laugh.

"I guess Pete's mother is still in town?" I asked.

"Yes, she's staying for a bit to help Lizzie and Mike with the kids and to go through Pete's belongings."

"That's good for the family," I said.

"It's wonderful for Lizzie," Rachel said. "I saw her in the mud pits, drinking cocktails with two of her friends as if she didn't have a care in the world."

"You can drink cocktails in the mud pits?" I queried. I shuddered at the potential for mess. What if you spilled your rum runner in the mud you were naked in? Yuck.

"Apparently," Rachel replied. "I mean, I know it must be hard for her to be stuck at home with three kids day in and day out, but she chose that path. If she really wanted to be a singer, she should have made different choices instead of sitting home and resenting everyone else's freedom."

I wondered if Rachel and Keith were childless by choice, but I wasn't rude enough to ask. For a brief moment, I wished Skye were here. She was willing to ask the questions other people weren't. That was why she made a good reporter, not that I'd ever admit it to her.

"I'm sorry I seem so difficult. Thank you for being so flexible," Rachel said. "I know it can't be easy, juggling all these personalities."

"It's part of the job," I said brightly.

Rachel scraped back her chair and stood. "I need to get back to the band. Kyle Charney needs *a lot* of practice before he's ready. It's tough bringing in a new member so last minute. It could ruin our chances."

"Well, Pete couldn't exactly help dying," I said. "I'm sure he would've opted for a different outcome."

Rachel's expression darkened. "Of course. I wasn't suggesting otherwise. Keith and I are devastated. Life won't be the same without Pete." She inhaled deeply and hoisted her bag over her shoulder. "I'll see you at the competition, ladies."

I RETURNED HOME FROM EVIAN'S OFFICE AND TRIED TO focus. I sat on the couch and stared at my bulleted list for the hundredth time, burning the tasks into my corneas. I knew it was partly stress—because I was always stressed—but there was also a sadness that lingered. I'd thought confessing to Lucas the morning after karaoke was the right thing to do, but now I wasn't so sure. His reaction had been much worse than I anticipated. Our pranks occurred more than a decade ago and he'd grown into a successful, confident man. I had no idea that our behavior had scarred him so deeply. I felt terrible.

You haven't eaten for hours, miss, Gerald commented. *Shall I fix you something?*

I shook my head, the lump in my throat prevented me from answering.

Is this about the murder? Gerald asked. *Why are you blocking your thoughts from me?*

I offered my familiar a reassuring smile. "It's not you, Gerald. I'm just having a moment." The truth was that I felt ashamed and I didn't want Gerald to know. He thought the world of me and if he knew how much I'd hurt Lucas, however unintentionally, I didn't want that to change his opinion of me. Gerald was more than my familiar—something Stuart failed to grasp—the armadillo was a part of me.

Is this about the conversation you had with Master Luke the other day on the porch? he pressed.

"Don't push it, Gerald," I said. "And don't call him Master Luke."

Apologies, miss. I meant no offense. You're both fans. I wasn't mocking him.

"I know you weren't," I replied. "You're better than that. Always better." And he made me a better witch as a result. That was another thing Stuart didn't understand. Gerald didn't simply shower me with cups of tea and read my innermost thoughts. He also served as my spiritual guide. My moral compass. I sometimes lacked the maturity of other women my age, which was odd considering I'd been left to my own devices since I was a teenager. Since the coven had abandoned us. You'd think I'd have grown up faster, but instead, I seemed to have stalled.

Forgive me, miss, but I believe Jane Austen is trying to draw your attention.

My chin jerked up. Sure enough, the eyes of my marble bust of Jane Austen glowed red. "You've got to be kidding me! Not now."

Jane Austen's bust was my charmed object that acted as a direct line to the coven. Her glowing red eyes meant only one thing — an incoming call from the mainland. I bet I knew why they were calling, too. I'd thank Skye in person with a friendly hex the next time I saw her.

I walked over to the bust and tugged her ear. "Good morning, Hestia. To what do I owe the pleasure?"

"I'm surprised to catch you at home," Hestia replied. "It sounds as though you have a lot on your plate. I should think you'd be out and about, cleaning up whatever mess it is that you've made."

I stiffened. "I don't know what you've heard, but I'm not responsible for any mess. This isn't St. Joan's." Hestia was my coven mentor. She'd fled the island along with the rest of the coven after the Incident That Shall Not Be Named. We didn't exactly have a close, personal relationship. It was hard to have such a thing with the witch who basically abandoned me to my fate. Unfortunately, she was also my only link to the mainland and coven headquarters.

"How's Trixie?" she asked. "Have you seen her?" Trixie was Hestia's familiar, a black cat with white paws that refused to leave the island when the witches evacuated. She ran with Tut's crowd in the forest and I only saw her on occasion.

"As far as I know, she's doing well," I said. "I've seen Tut recently, and I'm sure he would've mentioned it if there were any issues."

"You mean issues like winged monkeys?"

I closed my eyes in frustration. "Who told you about them?" I bet Skye didn't contact Hestia directly. That was too obvious. She probably blabbed to her mentor, Jadis. Skye knew perfectly well that Jadis would go straight to Hestia with the news. Those witches on the mainland had nothing better to do than micromanage life on the island. If they cared so much, they should have stayed. "Skye and her big mouth are going to be sorry. She knows I'm already in the middle of a crisis."

Hestia paused. "What other crisis?"

Magic and mayhem, me and my big mouth. Word obviously hadn't reached the coven about Pete's murder, most likely because it wasn't magic related. "Nothing. Just a scheduling conflict. You know how important schedules are to me."

"I certainly do, Kenna. Anyway, it doesn't matter how I know about the creatures," Hestia said. "The only thing that matters is sending those freaks of nature back where they belong. Please tell me you have a plan."

"Of course," I said. "When do I not have a plan? I'm the Queen of Plans." That much was true, and I typically executed them well. In this case, I felt slightly over my head. I think it was the combination of Pete's murder and Lucas that was throwing me off my game.

"Are you sure, Kenna?" I detected a note of concern in

Hestia's voice. Well, it was too late for her concern. She'd lost that privilege when she left. She was a fire witch like me. I could have learned so much more from her, if only she'd stayed. Now I was left to teach myself, along with whatever Gerald could research for me. I was lucky to have him.

"Everything is under control," I insisted. "The island will be a monkey-free zone soon enough. I'm not going to do anything to jeopardize the Battle of the Bands competition. I've worked too hard on it."

"I knew that would be the ideal job for you there," Hestia said. Jane Austen smiled, reflecting my mentor's delight. "I still remember when you started in the tourism office. I knew you'd be successful there. You've managed to hone your organizational skills to benefit the community. You should be proud, Kenna."

"I don't need your approval, but thanks," I said. Generally speaking, I was proud. Right now, I felt as if my whole world was caving in. It was like St. Joan's all over again, and if I didn't get things under control quickly, another cataclysmic event would change everything. I couldn't afford to go through that again. That was the reason I needed order. And control. I knew my coven sisters made fun of me for those traits, but they were a necessity. Gerald was right—I wasn't able to cope without them.

"I also heard that you've been seen around town with a rather attractive young man," Hestia said. "Anything you'd care to share with me?"

"Dream on," I said. Hestia wasn't my confidante. She didn't deserve to share the private details of my life.

"I'm not asking as your bestie," Hestia said. "I'm asking as a high-ranking member of this coven. You have to consider Eternal Springs, Kenna. It can't be all about you."

If she'd been standing in front of me, I would have set her

hair on fire. "All I do is think about Eternal Springs. It's literally my job to put this town first."

"I realize that, but getting involved with a local man..." She trailed off, clearly trying to choose her words carefully. "It's difficult to be close to someone without revealing your true nature. If he were to discover the truth, it could be problematic for you, for the coven, and for all of Eternal Springs."

"So I guess I should have become a nun after all," I griped.

"That's not what I'm suggesting." Hestia paused. "Okay, maybe it's not the worst idea in the world, but you can't put your own happiness ahead of the fate of the island. The residents have no clue what lurks on the other side. Without you four to maintain the balance..."

My frustration spilled out of me. "I don't see how dating Lucas puts the whole island in danger."

"How do you think Lucas would react if he knew you were a witch? If he saw you battling a flying monkey or hurling a fireball? Do you think he'd take it in stride? That the two of you would have a good laugh about it and then go for a coffee afterward?"

I plucked Jane Austen's neck and hurt my fingers on the marble in the process. "Maybe."

"Even if Lucas was willing to accept your identity, do you think the rest of Eternal Springs would be so open-minded?" Hestia challenged me. "Can you see Buddy embracing the four of you as the champions of Eternal Springs?"

No, *that* I could not envision. At all.

"I get your point," I grumbled. "Witches equal angry townsfolk with pitchforks. I'll bear it in mind."

"Very well then," Hestia said. "Please be sure to report back once you've handled the situation. I don't need to explain to you the importance of keeping those flying monkeys out of sight. It would cause more chaos than even you could handle, Kenna."

"Thanks for the vote of confidence," I said, and yanked on Jane Austen's ear to end the call.

Gerald looked at me. *Well?*

"Fire up the stove, Gerald. I'm going to need a bowl of oatmeal to power through the rest of this day." I paused. "Throw in some raisins and cinnamon, too."

Gerald appeared shocked. *Extra sugar, miss? Are you quite sure?*

I gave him a firm look. "Do it."

Chapter Sixteen

With my stomach full of oatmeal and my head clear of chaos, I was ready to tackle the items on my task list when the doorbell rang.

I'm afraid it's Master...Lucas Holmes, miss, Gerald said.

My stomach plummeted. Was he here to berate me, now that he'd had time to process what I'd revealed? I didn't blame him, really.

Thankfully, I was ready to face any challenge the universe threw my way. I gathered my courage and opened the door.

"Hi, Lucas," I said. I didn't smile, in case he was here to ream me out.

Although his hands were thrust in his pockets and his hair was slightly ruffled, he didn't appear angry.

"Is this a bad time?" he asked.

"Not for you," I replied. "I'm sorry about…"

He held up a hand. "I overreacted, Kenna. What you did…It happened more than ten years ago. It doesn't matter now."

"It was mean and it hurt you."

"But you confessed," Lucas said. "You didn't have to tell me. I never would've known."

"Yeah, that was pretty stupid of me, huh?"

A slow grin emerged. "You're a lot of things, but stupid isn't one of them."

"So, you forgive me?" I asked. I didn't know why it was so important to me, but it was.

"On one condition," he said.

Uh oh. I dearly hoped it had nothing to do with karaoke. "What is it?"

"Do you trust me?"

I hesitated. "That depends. Trust you in what way? To do my taxes? Probably not." Unless he was also a licensed tax professional, which, at this point, I'd be willing to believe. Lucas seemed capable of anything.

He laughed. "That's a lawyer answer. You're not secretly a lawyer, are you? I might have to rethink this relationship."

Relationship? That was a heavy word.

Lucas must have sensed my thought because he quickly said, "Friendship, I mean." He reached into his pocket and pulled out a handkerchief. "If you do, put this on."

I stared at the blue-and-white striped handkerchief. "Put this on? You mean fold it into a square and place it in my shirt pocket?" Because I didn't have one.

"You're not going to make this easy, are you?" He positioned the handkerchief like a blindfold. "I'm going to secure this around your head, so that you can't see where were going. Now do you get it?"

I got it. Lucas wanted to blindfold me and take me to an undisclosed location. Serial killer 101. But I knew Lucas wasn't a serial killer. He was the kindest, most compassionate man I'd ever known. It helped that his hotness was off the charts.

Hestia's words of warning rang in my ears, but I blocked

her out. Hestia wasn't living a life on this island, dedicated to protecting its inhabitants. *I* was.

"I trust you, Lucas." I really did. He'd shown me over and over again that I could, and it was time that I listened to my gut.

He tied the handkerchief around my head and took my hand. I felt the electricity between us. I hoped my powers didn't suddenly develop a mind of their own or Evian's *Firestarter* comments would cease to be a joke.

Lucas guided me down the front porch steps to his golf cart in the driveway.

"Sit back and relax," he said. "It's not a far drive. I'd say enjoy the scenery, but I guess I'll just have to describe it to you." And he did. The entire ride, Lucas provided running commentary on everything we passed. He was funnier than I realized. He was also observant. When he made a crack about Mrs. Atwood's outfit always matching that of her Yorkshire terrier's, I burst into laughter.

"I thought I was the only one who noticed that," I said.

"How could anyone *not* notice?" Lucas asked.

When the golf cart slowed to a stop, I actually felt disappointed. I liked listening to his voice as he entertained me. He wasn't trying to get me to organize or schedule anything. In fact, I felt that the only thing he wanted in the world right now was to make me laugh. It was a nice change.

"Right this way, Miss Byrne," he said, taking my hand again. I could get used to all this handholding.

He had me step up—it seemed higher than a normal step and narrower.

"Get comfortable," he said, "and I'll be around to remove your blindfold in a few minutes."

I heard unfamiliar sounds and the click of a door, then seatbelts. Seatbelts? There was only one mode of transport on the island I could think of that involved a seatbelt.

"Lucas," I said slowly. "Are we on a plane?"

"Two more minutes and I'll answer your question," he said.

Magic and mayhem, we were on a plane! Panic rose in my throat and threatened to spread to the rest of my body. It wasn't simply the act of flying that concerned me, it was also the fact that I wasn't allowed to leave the island. None of the witches could. I had no idea what would happen. What if there was a protection spell that crashed the airplane? What if Lucas was hurt because of me? The idea was too much to bear.

"Lucas!" I whipped off the handkerchief to object, but it was too late. The first thing I noticed were the clouds around us. How had he managed to take off without me noticing?

"See? You're perfectly safe," he said.

"But how?" I gripped the edge of my seat, straining my knuckles. "I didn't feel anything when we took off. I thought my stomach would do somersaults or something."

"I tried to take it easy," Lucas said, "so as not to frighten you." He glanced over at me. "I want this to be a positive experience for you."

"Why?" I couldn't bring myself to look down. Knowing the clouds were around me was bad enough.

"Because I'm hoping you'll want to do it again."

"Why do you want me to fly?" I asked. "I'm not a pilot."

"Because flying is my passion, Kenna," he said. "And, truth be told, so are you. I'd like to be able to bring my two passions together."

My grip relaxed slightly. "I'm...your passion?" I'd never been anyone's passion before. Heck, I hadn't even been anyone's girlfriend before.

"That's why I was so upset when you told me about the Darth Vader prank," he confessed. "I wouldn't have been so bothered if you were some random girl from high school, but it was *you*. You were my Charlie Brown football, constantly slipping through my grasp. I tried so many times to work up the courage to approach you, but I never felt good enough. You always seemed so cool and in control."

"So are you," I said. "You fly planes for a living. You can't do that without being cool and in control, right?"

"It's not the same," he replied. "You basically herd cats for a living. That's so much harder than what I do. I only need to rely on myself, for the most part. You have to deal with groups of people." He shuddered. "That's completely outside my wheelhouse."

"Where are we now?" I asked.

"Take a look and see," he said. "Go on. You won't fall out." He paused. "Unless I open the door and kick you."

I jerked toward him. "Lucas!"

He laughed heartily. "I would never hurt you, Kenna. Not ever. You can trust that, too."

I stared into those blue eyes and knew that it was true. I drew a relaxing breath and looked out the window. Below us was a huge body of water and the northern end of the island. I could tell it was north because of the white caps.

It was insanely beautiful.

"Peaceful, isn't it?" he asked softly.

"It's so serene," I agreed. And nothing happened to me. I was hundreds of feet in the air and nothing tried to pull me back to earth. It seemed that the coven trusted us enough to stay without the need of a protective spell. Good to know.

We circled the island a few times and Lucas pointed out places of interest. It was exhilarating to view the island from a different vantage point.

"I can't believe this is your job," I said. "If this is your passion, you must feel like the luckiest guy in the world."

He gave me a shy smile. "Almost, but not quite. There is the matter of that elusive football."

I smiled back. "I'm not sure that I like being compared to a scrap of leather."

He cocked an eyebrow. "Would you rather I compare you to a white whale?"

"You wouldn't dare." I couldn't believe what was happening. The guy I had been lusting after just told me that I was the missing piece of his happiness puzzle. I'd been chasing after waffles, while he'd been pursuing something far more meaningful. I didn't feel worthy of him.

"So you've forgiven me?" I asked.

"You were young," he said. "So was I. I like to think we've both matured since then."

"You don't play with your lightsaber in the forest anymore?" I teased. "That's a bit of a disappointment. I was hoping we might play together one day."

His grin widened. "We don't need to be on the ground to play *Star Wars*," he said. He adjusted his headset and focused on the sky in front of us. "I have the Death Star in my sights, Captain. Permission to fire."

"Are we in an X-wing fighter?" I asked.

He cast me a sidelong glance. "What else?"

In the middle of our game of destroy the Death Star, I caught sight of something below us, skimming the treetops. I may have been airborne, but the sight of the winged monkeys brought me plummeting back to earth.

I cast a sidelong glance at Lucas to see if he'd noticed. Thankfully, his attention was on the controls.

"A Star Destroyer ahead," I said.

Lucas played along. As long as I could keep his attention away from the monkeys below, we'd pass over them quickly.

"A clean shot," he cried, delighted.

I laughed. Lucas was so much fun to be around. I'd forgotten what it felt like to have fun for the sake of it. Most of my life centered around work engagements. Events that benefitted the island first, me second. Spending time with Lucas was purely for me and it was heavenly.

As much as I was enjoying myself, though, it was time to return to the island. I had to deal with those monkeys before they captured another dog. To say I was disappointed to end our outing was an understatement.

I wasn't even nervous when Lucas landed the plane. Unsurprisingly, he made an expert landing. Not even a bump out of place.

"So, what's the verdict?" he asked, regarding me.

"That was the most fun I've ever had in my life," I said.

"I'm so glad," Lucas said. "Now put the blindfold back on."

I wrinkled my nose. "Why? What's the point?"

"You look better with it on," he teased. "I can see much less of your face."

I jabbed him with my elbow. "Not funny!"

He couldn't contain his gleeful laughter. "Has anyone ever told you that you're fun to tease?"

I frowned. "No one's ever tried before." I knew why, too. It was because I always seemed so serious. Well, Lucas got a glimpse of the real me—not the witch or the tourism director but the person—and he wasn't running. My body warmed from the inside out.

"Thanks for this, Lucas," I said. "You have no idea how much it means to me."

He gazed at me with those bright blue eyes. "Ditto."

After my flight with Lucas and his offer of forgiveness, I felt reinvigorated and ready to take on the trio of winged monkeys. It was as if I'd surmounted a mental barrier.

I rode my scooter to the forest with Stuart flying above

me. His job was to locate the terrible trio. As multitalented as Gerald was, he couldn't possibly fly high enough to perform reconnaissance. Not until he lost weight. I made him stay behind for his own safety. He promised to have a pot of tea waiting when I returned.

"I see them," Stuart cried, swooping close to my head.

"Personal space, Stuart," I said. "Where are they?"

"If I tell you, can I be your new familiar?"

"No," I said firmly. "But you will have my eternal gratitude."

"I'll take it. They're back near the copse," Stuart said.

They were tormenting the sarcastic trees again? Those monkeys did not learn boundaries. If they were children, they'd be spending some serious time on the naughty step.

"Thanks, Stuart." I steered in the direction of the Cottonmouth Copse.

"What can I do now?" he asked eagerly.

"Just stay out of the way," I said. "I don't want you to get hurt."

"It's my job to protect you," Stuart insisted.

I parked far enough away from the copse so as not to alert the monkeys to my presence. "It's not your job at all. You owe me nothing, Stuart."

"Go get 'em, Kenna!" Stuart cried and flew off.

I took a few deep, cleansing breaths before heading into the copse. Sure enough, the winged monkeys were there, jumping up and down on branches and making a general nuisance of themselves.

"I hope you're here to take care of this, witch," Agatha said. "You've let it go on long enough."

"You're right, Agatha, and I'm sorry."

The three monkeys took to the air and began circling me.

"You'll pay for making us itch," the alpha monkey said. "I have scabs from scratching too hard."

"At least they're an improvement on your appearance," I said.

"Look out, Kenna," Earl cried.

I jumped back as the alpha monkey swiped at me with a deadly claw.

"Don't you lay a hand on my witch," Stuart cried.

"I'm not *your* witch, Stuart." Did I really need to deal with Stuart's exuberance now?

It was then that I realized Stuart was above us in a dive-bomb position, plummeting straight for the alpha monkey. There was no way he'd win in a fight with any one of the monkeys, let alone the alpha.

"Stuart, no!" I shouted.

The alpha monkey bared his teeth, and I watched as he extended his claws, waiting for Stuart to come within range. I had to do something *now*.

One of the fire spells from the spell book flashed in my mind. I poured my magic into my fingertips and recited, "For this situation dire, manifest a lasso of fire." I extended my hand and a flaming rope appeared. I swung it over my head, making sure the loop was wide enough to encircle all three monkeys. I couldn't risk any one of them escaping. I yanked hard and tightened the lasso so that the three monkeys slammed together and fell to the ground.

"The rope..." the alpha monkey grimaced. "It burns!"

Smoke billowed from their bodies. I didn't want to kill them, only to send them back where they belonged. I ran toward them, still clutching the end of the lasso. I couldn't afford to douse the flames until I'd finished the job.

"Are you going to roast us and eat us?" the second monkey asked.

"That's disgusting," I said.

"When I get my claws in you," the alpha monkey spat, "I'll start with your big mouth."

I scrunched my nose. "You're going to eat my mouth first? That doesn't even make sense. My mouth is a gaping hole."

"You've got that right," Agatha interjected.

I ignored her and spread my arms as though I were embracing the trio. "Three creatures without a soul. Return them to their demonic hole."

The wind blew so hard around us, that even the sarcastic trees bent to its will.

"My leaves," Myra cried. "I'm naked without my leaves!"

"You're naked without your bark," Agatha countered. "Your leaves are like accessories."

"Ah, good point," Myra replied.

The wind whipped around us. Even Stuart sought refuge at the base of Earl's trunk.

"Puppies," the second monkey wailed. "We only wanted puppieeeeeees!"

Their wings melted first, followed by their hairy brown bodies. With a final howl of despair, they disappeared into the dirt.

I stared at the circle of scorched earth, checking that they were truly gone before relinquishing my fiery lasso. One flick of my fingers and it vanished.

"Are they dead?" Stuart asked, flying over to investigate.

"No," I replied. "I've only sent them back to the other side, the place they came from."

"You saved me." Stuart gazed at me in amazement. "You like me. You really like me."

"I didn't just save you, Stuart," I said. "I saved the puppies of Eternal Springs."

"And us," Earl said. "Don't forget us."

"That magic lasso was killer," Stuart said. "I've never seen you use fire like that before."

It was then that the realization hit me. I had used fire—a real fire spell, not some watered-down version—and I'd used it well. "Thanks, Stuart. It feels...good." It really did. I felt more like myself than I had in ages.

"You, my dear, are a badass," Myra pronounced.

"It's one thing to send them back to their hellhole, but who's going to clean up all their poop?" Agatha asked.

"You're never satisfied," Myra said.

"Maybe my standards are just higher than yours," Agatha shot back.

"Your branches aren't even higher than mine," Myra retorted smugly.

At least they were turning on each other and not on me. "I'll see what I can do about the monkey poop. In the meantime, I have a murder to solve and a band competition to run."

I returned to the clearing where my scooter awaited me, a swagger in my step.

I was ready to rock.

Chapter Seventeen

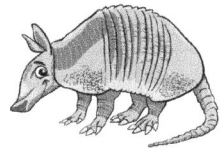

The time is nigh, Gerald called.

I bolted upright in bed. Streaks of sunshine invaded my bedroom. Another sunny day. Yes! I punched the air. Perfect weather for a Battle of the Bands competition on the beach.

Thanks for waking me, I said.

I'm downstairs and breakfast is on the table.

I flipped the covers back just enough so that I could slide out without messing up the bedding. *I'll be right there.* I wanted to be the first to arrive at Anchors Away and the last one to leave. That was the only way to make sure the event went smoothly from start to finish.

I came downstairs to a steaming bowl of oatmeal and banana drizzled with honey.

One of your favorites, miss.

"Gerald, this is so sweet," I said. "I know you'd rather have eggs and bacon."

You'll need a healthy breakfast for the long day ahead.

I pointed my spoon at him. "And this is why Stuart will never unseat you, not that it's possible anyway."

You and I have a long history together, Gerald said. *It isn't a simple matter of companionship.*

"Too right." I devoured my oatmeal and gulped down the cup of tea that Gerald had also prepared. It had just the right amount of milk and sugar.

I don't suppose you want me along for moral support. Gerald gave me a hopeful look.

"You know I'd love that, but hundreds of people dancing and drinking...I'm afraid you'd get trampled, especially when you'd have to hide your wings and not fly."

Very well then. Gerald heaved a sigh. *At least Master Lucas will be there to support you.*

I sucked down the last of my tea. "Lucas and I haven't actually discussed it, but I assume he'll be there. Goddess knows he's spent enough time flying people to the island for it."

You've been much more relaxed since you left with him yesterday.

"I feel more relaxed."

Do you think he'll be around more often now?

I swallowed the last spoonful of oatmeal and looked at my pink fairy armadillo. "Are you concerned, Gerald?"

Concerned, miss?

I brought my empty bowl and cup to the kitchen sink. "You sound like you might be concerned about Lucas coming around. Are you worried about our secret?"

I suppose it's a bit of that. He fluttered to the sink, his bottom dipping to the floor the entire distance.

"We're on the same page then," I said. "I'm worried, too. Hestia has a point. I'm used to hiding my identity from people, but I've never been close enough to anyone to care."

Maybe that's the reason you haven't, Gerald suggested. *You know it will be an issue at some point.*

"Superman didn't have these problems," I said. "Lois Lane was thrilled to be with Superman. I'm not sure Lucas would feel the same way about dating a witch." It would be like Luke finding out Darth Vader was his father. Okay, maybe not that bad, but still.

Stuart is the other part of it, Gerald confessed.

I laughed. "Gerald, you know perfectly well that you don't need to worry about Stuart replacing you. It will never happen."

But he doesn't give up, Gerald said. *And he's forever breathing down my neck, waiting for me to misstep. It's most unpleasant.*

"I can see how that might be stressful." I headed upstairs to shower and change. Gerald trailed behind me. "What if we offered Stuart an official role?"

A witch cannot have two familiars, Gerald protested. *It simply isn't the done thing.*

"No, not as a familiar," I said. Stuart had proven himself loyal and useful recently. He deserved something for his efforts. "Maybe there's a reference in the coven handbook. Some antiquated position he can have. That might get him off your back."

Or I could cast a protective spell around the house.

"I'd rather not. Those have a way of backfiring," I said. I turned on the shower. "You can research it today while I'm at Anchors Away."

I shall draw you a hot bath upon your return.

"Thanks, Gerald. You're the best."

And don't you forget it, miss.

While I wasn't the first person to arrive at Anchors Away, I was close enough. I was pleased to note multiple bartenders behind the bar instead of just one. My pleas for additional staff had not fallen on deaf ears.

Equipment was strewn across the sand as the sound crew prepared to set up for the competition.

"Things are moving along. It's going to be a great day, Kenna." Mack gave me a thumbs up from behind the bar.

"Thanks, Mack," I called. "Knock wood for me."

He made a big show of knocking on the palm tree that jutted from the middle of the bar.

"Um, I don't mean to nitpick, but, technically, a palm tree is a type of grass."

Mack quickly knocked on the bar top instead. I spent the next hour running around like a preschool teacher, admonishing grown men for infantile and dangerous acts and desperately trying to keep everyone on task before the spectators arrived. Once the stage and speakers were ready, I ventured out to the beach where the bands' trailers were lined up. The trailers were smaller than average because they had to be pulled by golf carts. I counted the correct number of trailers and breathed a sigh of relief. So far, so good.

The venue finally opened and spectators poured in. I couldn't believe how many people were already here.

"You've outdone yourself this time, Kenna," Buddy said, ambling his way toward me. Mitzi walked beside him, dressed as if she were headed to a Vegas nightclub.

"Thank you, Buddy," I said.

"Hopefully, that drummer's death won't overshadow the event," Mitzi said, unhelpfully.

"No one's talking about it now that they know it was drug-related," Buddy said.

I resisted the urge to argue. I had to keep Buddy on my good side, especially today.

"I'm sure it will be fine," I said. Except for the simple fact that the killer was still at large.

I heard Evian's voice as she introduced the first band. The crowd cheered. It was the perfect excuse to extricate myself from Buddy.

"I'll talk to you when it's quieter," I yelled over the din. I maneuvered my way through the bodies and stopped by the bar to check on Mack.

"Hey, Kenna," Mack greeted me. "So far, so good, right? These four fellas here are from a place called Spellbound. Isn't that a funny name for a town?"

My mouth nearly dropped open. To the naked eye, they looked like four regular young men. As a witch, I could see right through their glamours to the paranormals they really were.

Once I gathered my wits, I asked, "Which band?"

"Look Mom, No Wings," one guy replied. An elf. His glamour required the least amount of magic because the only paranormal part of him was his pointy ears.

"Where's Spellbound?" I asked.

"Pennsylvania," he said. "Near the Poconos."

"This our first East Coast tour," another guy said. Beneath his glamour was a huge set of wings. "We're really excited to see new places."

"Welcome to Eternal Springs," I said. "And good luck today."

"Can I get you a drink?" Mack offered.

"Not now, thanks," I said. "I'm just making sure everything's running smoothly."

"There you are." Lucas stood before me in all his manly perfection.

"You're wearing a shirt," I said.

Lucas grinned. "Is that disappointment or relief I hear?"

I dodged the question. "They're good, right?"

"Not too shabby," he said. "Have you had anything to eat or drink yet? Why do I get the feeling you've been going nonstop since you woke up?"

"I ate breakfast," I said. "Gerald made me oatmeal." The words were out of my mouth before I could stop them. Lucas was so easy to talk to that it was hard to keep my guard up.

Lucas laughed. "Your armadillo made you breakfast? Now there's a trick I'd like to see."

I smiled, as though I'd meant to be funny. "You should see how he makes the bed. Perfect hospital corners."

Lucas gave my shoulder an affectionate squeeze. "I like that you're so calm right now. This is your big event and you're cracking jokes. I love it."

"Kenna? Cracking jokes? That doesn't sound right." Skye elbowed her way through the crowd to stand beside Lucas. "Maybe someone's cast an opposite spell on her."

I narrowed my eyes at her. "If only there was such a thing. I'd use it on you in a heartbeat."

Lucas appeared thoroughly amused. "You two fight like sisters."

"Good thing we're not related or I might have been stuck with that same sour expression," Skye said.

I gave her an exaggerated smile. "Why don't you focus on covering the event, Skye? At least I'm providing your readers with something that might actually interest them for a change."

Skye stuck out her tongue before continuing to push her way through the crowd.

Fat Gandalf was third, as Rachel had demanded, and it was during their set that I noticed Zola get passed over the top of the mosh pit. I wondered how many rum runners she'd already sucked down. The day had barely begun.

On a trip to the ladies room after my third sparkling water, I bumped into Lizzie. She stood in front of the mirror, applying a bright coat of coral lipstick.

"How do I look?" she asked, smoothing the front of her sparkling mini-dress.

"Much better than I would after having three kids," I said truthfully. That body did not look like it had housed three babies.

Lizzie gave her reflection a satisfied smile. "I'm on next."

"You are?" I mentally scanned the list. "I don't remember seeing your name."

"I'm joining the Temperamental Toddlers. Their lead singer thinks we harmonize really well together."

I'm sure he's thinking they'd do other things well together, too. I couldn't imagine Mike would be too pleased about it.

"Is your husband here?" I asked. "He must be excited to see you perform."

Lizzie's jaw tightened. "Mike's working, of course. Barb is home with the kids, so that I could come here." She flipped her long hair over her shoulder. "This is my big shot and I'm not missing out because some idiot has a circuit breaker problem."

Okay then. Lizzie had all the charm of Cruella De Vil. It wouldn't surprise me in the least if she sauntered onstage in a coat made of puppy fur.

"How long will your mother-in-law be in town?" I asked.

"Not long enough," Lizzie snapped. "She came for the funeral and seems ready to run back to Baltimore. I don't understand why she wouldn't want to spend more time with her grandchildren. God knows I spend enough time raising them."

Yikes! I didn't have kids, but that didn't seem like the best attitude for a mother. Maybe I'd feel differently if were in her position...but I hoped not.

"It sounds like you don't have the chance to get out much," I said. "Do you ever hire a babysitter so you can go to a class or meet up with friends?"

"Mike won't allow it," she said. "He says we need to save the money for the kids' college funds. With his mom in Baltimore and my parents in Denver, there's no one around."

"What about Tiffany?" I asked. "She might like to spend

more time with the kids now that Pete's gone. It's another connection to him."

Lizzie snorted. "My kids aren't made of metal. That's the only way they'd interest Tiffany. The worst part is they don't even nap anymore. I get zero breaks until Mike comes home."

A thought occurred to me. "So were you home with the kids the day Pete died?"

"Of course. Where else would I be?" She shimmied her shoulders and adjusted her cleavage. "There. That's better. Time to go. Wish me luck!"

"Good luck," I said weakly.

I had no doubt that Lizzie was telling the truth. Three little alibis and no nap schedule meant there was no way she could have murdered Pete in the bathroom here. Not a stone-cold killer then, just a stone-hearted package of unpleasantness.

Lizzie Simpson may have the voice to win the competition, but she was certainly no prize.

I left the bathroom and headed for the bar to get another bottle of water. On my way, I was straining to listen to Lizzie and the band when I bumped into a man with the best handlebar mustache I'd ever seen.

"You're Miss Byrne, aren't you?" he said.

"I am."

"You've done a marvelous job here," he said. "I've been to other competitions like this, but yours has been top of the heap."

"Thank you so much." I shook his hand. "Are you in a band?"

"Elvis have mercy, no," he said. "I'm the manager for Pigs in Blankets. Felix Monroe."

"Nice to meet you, Felix."

"I worried the whole event would be overshadowed by

Pete's death," Felix said. "He would insist that the show must go on, though, so I'm glad to see that it is."

I angled my head. "You knew Pete?"

"Oh, yes," Felix said. "I guess there's no reason to keep it a secret any longer. He was going to join us as our new drummer."

"What?" I wasn't sure I'd heard him correctly.

"Pete signed with us," Felix said. "He was planning to quit Fat Gandalf after today and come on tour with us."

"What happened to your regular drummer?" I asked.

"He decided to retire after the competition. He doesn't want to tour anymore." Felix stroked the end of his mustache. "It's exhausting, I admit. I don't know how some of the older musicians manage. You have no idea how many bottles of ibuprofen we consume each year."

"Did Pete tell his bandmates?" I asked.

Felix shook his head. "He said he wanted to wait until after the competition, to keep up morale. He planned to tell them after the winners were announced."

So Pete was heading for the mainland whether Fat Gandalf won or not.

"When did he sign the contract?" I asked.

Felix blew out a breath, causing his mustache hairs to twitch. "The morning of his death, sadly. We met at my hotel. His wife was with him, and she was not too happy about it, let me tell you."

My radar pinged. "Tiffany was with him? What did she say?"

Felix looked thoughtful. "That he was making a mistake, but she'd support his decision."

"She never mentioned it when I spoke to her," I said.

"I guess she didn't think it mattered anymore," Felix said. "He's not going anywhere now. No point in upsetting his bandmates further. They sounded good earlier, all things considered."

"I guess you still need a drummer."

"We do, but it's not the end of the world." He smiled. "There are plenty of candidates here today. And I get to listen to them all, so thank you for that."

"Thanks for coming," I said. "Enjoy the rest of the competition."

Felix carried on walking, but I stood motionless, absorbing the information about Pete. Pete was leaving no matter what and Tiffany knew it—but she had an alibi for that morning. I'd checked it myself. There had to be a part of her story I was missing.

As I reached the bar, I heard people calling my name.

"Kenna! It's Kenna, everyone!"

I whirled around to see a few of the bands from karaoke night waving me over. I recognized the faces but didn't remember their names.

"It's the beautiful Kenna Byrne," one of the men said, sloshing his beer everywhere as he raised his glass. "Good job on all this."

"Come over and drink with us," another man beckoned. He patted the empty stool beside him. "We could use someone attractive to balance out the rest of us."

They seemed far too drunk for my liking. Planting myself in that middle of their alcoholic haze was a bad idea, no question.

One of them lunged toward me and gripped my arm. "Have a shot with us, doll."

"Doll?" I echoed.

"Are my guys being inappropriate?"

I craned my neck to see Felix behind me. "Not yet, but give it a second."

"No more drinks for the rest of the day," Felix told his band members.

"Why not?" a bald one complained. "It's not like we have to perform." He winked at me. "On stage, anyway."

Ugh. "I'll check on the radio coverage where it's safer." I motioned toward Evian near the stage, who was talking to Rachel. Uh oh. I'd better make sure Rachel wasn't trying to strong-arm Evian into unauthorized changes. I had the sense she could be a real pitbull when she wanted something.

"I'm so pleased to see Pete's wife here," Felix said. "It must be difficult for her, though."

I frowned. "Where do you see Tiffany?"

"There." He pointed to where I was already looking. "The icy blonde."

Tiffany was blond, but she wasn't the one talking to Evian.

"That's Rachel Simonson, the manager for Fat Gandalf," I said.

And that quickly, all the pieces fell into place.

"Excuse me," I said in a rush. "There's something I need to take care of."

"Um, it's *someone*, doll, and I'm right here," the bald guy said, holding a shot glass aloft.

Under my breath, I muttered an incantation and heard a scream of shock.

"Water," someone shouted.

I smiled to myself. It wasn't the first time I'd turned a fireball shot into an actual fireball.

"He's fine," Felix said. "Only a little burn on his upper lip."

I didn't bother to glance over my shoulder as I walked away.

Chapter Eighteen

By the time I reached the stage, Rachel was gone. I asked Evian what she'd wanted.

"She's still pestering me about playing Fat Gandalf songs," Evian said. "As if I'm not completely busy right now."

"Do you know where she went?" I asked.

"Not sure. She wasn't happy with me, though. She said something about complaining to Buddy about my lack of island spirit. I think she headed toward the beach."

"Thanks, Evian."

"Good job on the flying monkey problem, by the way," Evian said. "I heard they've been sent back."

"They have," I said. "I'll tell you about it later."

Evian's brow lifted. "Really? Like you'll stop by and hang out just for fun?"

I recognized that expression. Like me, Evian wanted to be appreciated as more than a witch, an island protector, and a radio station owner. She wanted to be appreciated as plain old Evian.

"Yes, I'll bring Gerald," I said. "He and Paul can catch up."

Evian lit up like a firework and I hurried to the beach to catch up with Rachel.

I saw her up ahead, trudging along the coastal path lined with tiki torches. Her back was straight and her stride determined. She gripped a bottle of prosecco in her hand, no doubt anticipating the band's big win.

"Rachel!" I called. When she turned around, I gave a friendly wave. May as well lure her into a false sense of security.

She stopped walking and faced me. "Is there a problem, Kenna?"

I hustled toward her, my shoes sinking into the sand. "You tell me."

She placed a hand on her hip. "What's that supposed to mean? Was your friend complaining about my radio station request? I mean, *come on*. Fat Gandalf should be on there every day."

I launched right into my accusation. There was no time to hesitate. I had a competition to run. "I thought you didn't love Pete."

"Pete?" she asked, perplexed. "Why are you asking me about Pete?"

"You told me you didn't love him, that night at Coconuts."

"I did? I must've been really drunk." She paused. "Not because I actually loved him, of course, but because I talked to you about it. I barely know you."

I kept the involvement of truth serum to myself.

"If you didn't love him, why were you so upset at the prospect of him leaving the island?"

"It wasn't about him leaving *me*," she scoffed. "It was him leaving the band. Fat Gandalf was about to have its big break. Do you know how long I've been waiting for this? He was going to ruin *everything*?" Her voice grew shrill. "All my hard work and he was going to leave *our* band for that giant mustache and his Pigs in Blankets."

Rachel had been telling the truth about one thing—her lack of romantic feelings for Pete. Despite their affair, it was clear that Rachel didn't care about Pete at all. She only cared about the success of the band she managed.

"Why did you need to kill him?" I asked, and saw her flinch. "Couldn't you have just hired another drummer?" The way Pigs in Blankets had hired Pete. "That's what you ended up having to do anyway."

She looked around us and back at me. I could see the wheels turning in her mind. We were the only two at this end of the beach. Everyone else was in the bar area, watching the performance.

"I had no desire to replace Pete," she said. "It takes ages to get the sound right. The drummer is the backbone of the band." The vein in her neck throbbed.

"Then what happened?" I asked. "Tell me, Rachel." Maybe it was an accident.

"I didn't intend to kill him. I was trying to talk him out of the deal with Pigs in Blankets, but he refused to rescind the contract." Her fingers tightened around the bottle of prosecco. "He tried to end the argument by going into the men's room, but I followed him in. Like a bathroom door could stop me."

"You were really angry," I said, more of a statement than a question.

"I was furious!" Her arms flailed. "I couldn't believe that he would betray me like that. We were supposed to be in this together."

"So you followed him into the bathroom," I said. "Then what happened?"

"I pretended that I understood his reasons and wanted to congratulate him properly." A vague smile tugged at her lips.

"That got him to open the stall door. He was always so easy to seduce."

Good Goddess, she was horrid.

"I swung the door hard and hit him in the head. He twisted and fell backward. Then his head slammed again on the toilet tank." Her eyes blazed with fury.

"Was he still alive?" I asked. He might have lived if she'd gotten help.

She shrugged. "I didn't bother to check. He slid down to the floor and collapsed, like a loser. I don't deal in losers, so I left. Good riddance to him."

When I looked into Rachel's steely eyes, I was shocked to see myself reflected there. The anger and resentment. The fiery passion that lurked beneath the surface. The need for organization and control. I understood her more than I cared to. There was one crucial difference.

"I have a heart," I said quietly.

"Congratulations," Rachel spat. "A shame it'll have to stop beating now. Can't have you telling the authorities what really happened."

"What's your plan?" I asked. "Because I can drink a whole bottle of prosecco, no problem. It won't kill me."

"The prosecco won't, but the glass might." Rachel smashed the prosecco bottle against the base of the nearest tiki torch. The bubbly liquid spilled out onto the sand. She brandished the broken bottle like a knife.

"Hey, someone has to clean that up," I yelled, pointing to the glass fragments in the sand.

"I don't like it any more than you do," she said. "But right now you're the bigger mess I need to clean up."

"You're insane," I said. "We're on a public beach. Someone will see you."

"Not if I finish you off quickly," she said. "One slice to the jugular and you'll bleed out right here. Could've been any one of those drunk men at the bar. Such cavemen." She gave a mock shudder.

"Stop right there," I commanded.

As she advanced toward me with the jagged bottle, I set the tiki torches ablaze.

Rachel's eyes bulged at the sight. "What? How did you do that?"

"Magic," I said and narrowed my gaze. "If I can do that to torches without touching them, imagine what I can do to you."

"You're bluffing," she said. "Nobody has that kind of power. They're probably set on a timer like my outdoor lights."

I pressed my hands firmly against my hips and gave her my most menacing stare. "Try me."

She crouched in a fighting stance, still clutching the broken bottle, and eyed me with a hardened expression. I had no doubt she'd kill me without remorse. Icy blonde, indeed.

"Show me another trick," Rachel taunted. "I bet that was pure luck."

I thought about the bottle in her hand. I couldn't take it by force, but I could try another way. I focused my magic on the broken bottle and recited an incantation under my breath. I felt the heat emanate from my fingers.

"Ouch! What the hell?" Rachel dropped the bottle and watched in disbelief as it dissolved into sand. "How?"

While she was distracted, I made my move. I lunged forward and tackled her to the ground. She fell backward and slammed her head into a sand dune. Too soft to knock her out. She kicked me to no avail. I held her wrists down firmly. I had no idea what to do now. I was too intent on her not getting the upper hand again.

"Don't burn me," she cried. "Please."

The sound of a motor was a relief. Buddy rolled to a stop

beside us, his golf cart covered in one of Mitzi's oversized knitted cozies. I didn't want to know how long that had taken her to make. I imagined hours of sleep after listening to that particular show.

"There you are, Kenna," he said. "Shouldn't you be overseeing the competition? Apparently, the lead singer for Last Man Standing is too drunk to perform."

I twisted my head toward him, still straddling Rachel. "Rachel killed Pete Simpson! It had nothing to do with drugs."

"I know that," Buddy said. "The toxicology report finally came back and his system was clean." He peered at Rachel's head, half buried in the sand. "So Keith's wife killed Pete?"

"I'm the band's *manager*, you idiot," Rachel spat, squirming to get out from under me. I had to admire her dedication to feminism.

"Could you maybe arrest her now, so I can get up?" I asked.

Buddy grinned. "I don't know. This is a mighty interesting situation."

"Buddy, we're not in the mud pits," I said.

Buddy looked disappointed. "Too bad."

"Please get her off me. She controls fire," Rachel shrieked, her eyes wild. "She's dangerous."

"I think you'll find you're the one who's dangerous," Buddy said, tossing me a set of handcuffs. He clucked his tongue. "This is what happens when they're wound as tightly as this one. They snap."

"I hope you're talking about people and not just women," I said.

Buddy shifted uncomfortably. "Naturally." He seemed to remember who he was talking to. "Present company excepted, of course."

I clicked one cuff around her wrist and guided her to the backseat, where I hooked the other cuff to the golf cart.

"Your chariot awaits, Rachel," I said, and hummed the theme song to *Chariots of Fire*. Her eyes widened with fright when she recognized the tune.

"Tell me who wins, would you?" Buddy asked amiably.

"Absolutely." Whoever won tonight, it sure wouldn't be Rachel.

She was still screaming about fire as Buddy's cart disappeared into the horizon.

SKYWALKER INCOMING. GERALD SOUNDED THE HIGH ALERT, fluttering around the house in a tizzy.

"You sound like Stuart," I said.

That's just insulting.

"Be nice. If he's going to be my new security detail, you two need to get along."

I stretched and got out of bed, still dragging from all the magic I'd used the night before. It drained me of more energy than I'd expected.

Gerald flew over with a brush in his mouth and dropped it on the bed beside me. *A necessity, miss.*

"Thanks, Gerald." I ran the brush through my hair and pulled out the tangles.

A knock on the door signaled his arrival. There was no time to change out of my pajamas. I splashed water on my face and hustled downstairs.

"Good morning, hometown heroine," he said. His hands were shoved in his pockets and he rocked back and forth on the balls of his feet.

"That's probably an overstatement," I said.

"Not to the rest of us. Everyone's talking about how you apprehended a cold-blooded murderer."

I blushed, despite my attempt to appear nonchalant. "I didn't have a choice. She was going to kill me." Death by prosecco, at least it would've been classy.

The way Lucas looked at me—my stomach dropped to my knees. No one had ever looked at me that way before. If I had to spend the rest of my life here, then I was going to do it on my own terms. That meant that if I wanted to play with Lucas's lightsaber, then, by golly, I was going to.

"Come outside," he said. "There's something I want you to see."

"Outside? But I'm in pajamas."

"So what? You look great. Then again, you look great in anything."

My heart soared as I followed him outside. Lucas was the kindest, sweetest…All thoughts came to a screeching halt when I saw what was parked on the street outside my house.

"The Waffle Wagon?"

Lucas grinned. "I tracked it all morning. When I told the owner who you are and that you were desperate for one of his famous waffles, he was only too happy to oblige."

I treaded carefully toward the wagon, as though it were a mirage. "You're amazing."

"Let's not lose sight of things," he said. "I captured a waffle. You captured a killer."

I stepped up to the Waffle Wagon and smiled. There was no need to place an order. All the waffles were the same—delicious liege Belgian waffles.

"For you, Miss Byrne," he said. "My name is Nicolaus and it's an honor to serve you."

"Thank you," I said. "You have no idea how long I've waited for this."

As I held the paper plate in my hands, the flapping of wings alerted me to a presence overhead.

"Take heed," Stuart cried. "I see cyanide all over that, my

esteemed mistress." With the swoop of a wing, he knocked the plate from my hands.

"That's powdered sugar," I said vehemently. I stared at the ground where the waffle had fallen face down on the concrete. I was ready to throttle that bird.

"It *is* sugar," Lucas said. "I thought that was half the appeal."

Of course, he couldn't understand Stuart. All he heard was the squawking of a deranged albino raven.

"Another one for you," Nicolaus said. "On the house."

Today felt like the luckiest day of my whole life. I bit into the warm waffle and sighed. It was every bit as wonderful as I'd imagined.

"Here," Nicolaus said, handing me a slip of laminated paper. "This is my schedule. I don't post it publicly, so keep it under your hat."

His schedule. The Waffle Wagon's schedule. My pulse raced. I examined the days and times as if admiring the Holy Grail. This was too good to be true.

I clutched the schedule to my chest. "You have no idea what this means to me," I said.

Nicolaus gave a friendly wave. "Glad you enjoy my waffles. Now I've got a schedule to keep. See you around." He pulled the Waffle Wagon back onto the road and drove away.

"Is it good?" Lucas asked.

"Amazing," I said, my mouth full of waffle. "Why didn't you get one?"

"I'm not big on sweets," he said.

I swallowed. "In that case, I'm not sure we can be friends."

Lucas fixed me with a hard stare. "Good, because I don't want to be friends."

Huh? I took a nervous bite of waffle. What had I done?

"You don't?" came my muffled response.

He gave a firm shake of his blond head. "Isn't it obvious? I want more than that with you, Kenna. I told you, you're my football."

Lucas didn't wait for me to swallow. He gripped my shoulders and pressed his lips against mine. Powdered sugar transferred from my mouth to his.

When we broke apart, I laughed. "That was probably messier than you were intending."

"That's okay," he said. "I like messy. More importantly, I like you."

"I...I..." I struggled to say the words. I liked him more than I ever thought possible. It was a new feeling for me—this helplessness against the rising tide of emotions.

Lucas flashed an anxious grin. "I'm on pins and needles here. Can you put me out of my misery?"

"May the Force be with you," Stuart called from the rooftop. If I'd had a stone in my hand, I would've chucked it at him.

"Would you like to go out to dinner tonight?" I blurted. "I can get us reservations at L'Etoile. They usually have tables available after eight on short notice."

Lucas chuckled. "Kenna, you don't have to plan this. In fact, I don't want you to. I'll organize everything. It'll be a surprise."

I grimaced. "A surprise?"

"Yes, I'll pick you up tonight at seven. Sound good?"

Good was an understatement. An evening alone with Lucas sounded like bliss. "No blindfolds?"

He pretended to be disappointed. "No shirt?"

I smiled. "As much I enjoy the view of your abs, restaurants generally require them."

"I was talking about yours, not mine."

I gave him a playful swat. "I'll go on one condition," I said, wiping the powdered sugar from my face.

"For you? Anything."

"Kiss me again," I said. "I had too much waffle in my mouth to enjoy it properly."

He pretended to roll up his sleeves. "I do take pride in my work."

"Work? Kissing me is work already? We've only just begun."

He grinned. "Promise?"

"Promise."

Also by Annabel Chase

To find out about new releases by Annabel Chase and receive a FREE bonus content, join my VIP List at www.annabelchase.com.

Other Books in the Elemental Witches of Eternal Springs series include—

Bat out of Spell by Amanda M. Lee

Spell on Earth by Leighann Dobbs

Spell or High Water by Gina LaManna

Other Series By Annabel Chase—

Starry Hollow Witches

Spellbound

Spellbound Ever After

The Bloomin' Psychic

Hex Support

Made in the USA
Middletown, DE
09 May 2025

75329645R00116